THE NAMELESS BREED

'Poor, bastard Texas!' Brazos said. 'Spain, Mexico, France, England . . . every country's slept with her. If ever there was a nameless breed, we're it!' The young Republic of Texas was poor, hungry and friendless, a prey to every adventurer. But Texans knew how to fight, and Brazos McCloud was a Texan. Trapped between agents of the greedy nations who were trying to plunder his country, Brazos got set to fight his way out, or die!

THE NAMELESS BREED

Will C. Brown

GUNSMOKE

WESTERNS

First published 1960
by
Macmillan

This hardback edition 1995
by Chivers Press
by arrangement with the author.
Reprinted by arrangement with
Golden West Literary Agency

ISBN 0 7451 4639 2

British Library Cataloguing in Publication Data available

Printed and bound in Great Britain by
Redwood Books, Trowbridge, Wiltshire

I

As the September dusk in San Antonio turned into a dark and shielding night, the stranger with the arrow wound decided that it was time to make his escape from the doctor's house.

He heard the *clop-clop* of the nine o'clock militia patrol fade toward Military Plaza. Eying the open window and the Texas night beyond, Brazos McCloud felt the need to know if the girl was now alone in the house and whether the doctor had gone out. He raised himself to his elbow and called, "Some water, please."

He heard her light footsteps. She came from the kitchen to his bedside and he accepted the gourd from her brown fingers.

"Your name, miss?" he asked. It seemed important.

"Risa."

He tried to study the lean sculpture of her profile but she turned away from the bed. Her attention was directed to his gun belt and holstered revolver hanging from a chair across the room.

Brazos McCloud drained the gourd. "Risa. That means laughter. But I haven't heard any laughter here."

"There isn't much to laugh at in a doctor's house. Do you need anything else?"

"Thank you, no. Has your father gone out?"

"Yes."

"Someone else was bitten by an arrow?"

He learned then that there was a little laughter in this house. He found it hiding behind her small-voiced reply. "This one's ailment is a little different from yours. A *puta* is having a baby."

He smiled. "It's one way to populate Texas."

"Yes. My father says the Republic is composed of nothing but mistakes."

An erect brown shadow, she moved to the light of the hallway, politely murmured, "Good night," and the door closed off the lamp rays.

Once through the window, Brazos steadied himself against the adobe wall to gain the feel of his legs. He pressed noise-

1

lessly along the house to the protection of the live oaks bordering Soledad Road and then shot across the open space in a soundless streak.

On the far side of the wagon ruts he took to the brush shadows. The night stretched peacefully around him and his face cooled to the touch of a fuzzy breeze. He drew his ribs deeply full, tasting the clean night with pleasure after the several days of medicine smells, during which he had learned that the Cherokee calling card in his shoulder had not amounted to much after all.

He could not say that he felt comfortable in this hodgepodge San Antonio. He chafed to get the transaction settled with Captain Spide and Trakken, and get out. His luck was stretched too thin. The militia might come searching for him any hour. He thought back to the holdup, days ago, and to the trail he might have left across eastern Texas. A part of his mind did the backtracking, looking for the mistakes, and another part worked ahead like a stalking redskin, sorting the small signs and instincts that helped a man stay alive when so many others were dying. He wanted to stay alive now. Life tasted better tonight than he had ever savored it before. *Wherever you are, Pa, we're trying to get there.* The biggest risk, he concluded, was whether the quiet girl back yonder happened to look under the bed mattress before he could return for the loot. That gamble was better than doing it the other way. Not that he liked it, but everything these days was a matter of choosing between bad gambles.

Without breaking his prairieman's stride, he swung his gun belt about his waist and buckled it. He emerged from the trees at the whispering river, crossed on the rocks below the Alamo's sad and brooding walls, and came out on a sandy path. This led to a stone house beyond the outskirts. He rapped heavily on the slab door and it opened a crack.

Trakken stood there, loosely holding a single-shot pistol. Brazos strode across the room, knew a flutter of weakness, and guessed that all the sap was not back in his legs yet. Trakken bolted the door.

"For God's sake, where have you been?"

Brazos touched his shoulder. "I picked up an arrow, here. Cherokees. They jumped me two hours out of Nacogdoches at the Angelina River. Then a wagon train picked me up, but I never knew it. This was days ago. I woke up in the doctor's house across town. He has a daughter. Risa. Such a girl!"

"Such a lie!" Trakken's mouth curled with suspicion.

"All right, you fool. Do you wish to see the blood crust?"

He dropped to a chair and noticed that his hands still had an unnatural paleness under the skin. "Be thankful I'm here and not a prisoner in the stockade. Why it is, Trakken, that one honest spy will not trust another honest spy? I'm new at this, you understand."

Trakken glided fitfully back and forth, crushing his knuckles. "Don't make me wait for the news until the Spider gets here." He stopped and hoarsely demanded, "Did you do it?"

Brazos answered with satisfaction. "I did. There was a robbery of the stagecoach across the Sabine. That was in Louisiana Territory, but the hue and cry will travel when it's found out what was taken."

"Yes, yes—go on! Did you get it?"

"A very strange robbery, they will say. Only one leather pouch stolen. From a government messenger of the United States." Brazos stopped. The size of his crime took shape in his mind.

With an effort, he continued to speak lightly. "I had the very hell of a time cutting the thing from the man's wrist. He bleated like I was carving off his manhood. But I got it. I would like to ask you, now, do you have my thousand dollars?"

"Captain Spide will attend to that."

Brazos shook his head. "The payoff part was with you, Trakken, not the Spider. I was to come here for my money."

"It's the same thing. It's all out of England's royal pocket. The news, man! Is the Union annexing Texas, or not?"

"I will be honest. I haven't read the documents yet."

"And why not?"

"The first two days I was in a high run, trying to put distance behind me. After that, there came the Cherokees. One runty buck was lucky to hit me, but unlucky in the end when I caught him in my rifle sight. So I dripped my blood all the way from the big timbers to San Antonio, bouncing in the settler's wagon like clabber in a churn."

Trakken sliced the air with an impatient gesture. "The messenger's pouch! Where is it?"

"I haven't seen the thousand dollars. And you have food in the kitchen, no doubt, and wine, but do you ask me if I might be hungry? Dr. Driscoll seemed to be long on whisky but short on rations. Where's your sympathy for a friend with a shoulder like a drawn beef quarter?"

"Very well!" Trakken said with icy formality. "You shall

eat. It gnaws me here," tapping his thin chest, "but I will bring the food and then I will wait until you have elected to tell me where *is* the cursed message from Washington!"

"Spoken like a gentleman." Brazos closed his hand over the pistol on the table. "I may be excused for admiring this while my back is turned to you and the kitchen. It is only that I am fond of firearms."

Trakken told him, "That is a poor joke."

Brazos ate wolfishly and washed the food down with warming gulps from a bottle of port.

"What's happened at this end while I've been gone?"

Trakken crushed his knuckles but maintained rigid control. "The question on everybody's tongue is the same. Is Sam Houston scheming with the Union to annex Texas, or will England pay him enough to keep us out? We feel positive that Washington was sending secret information to the United States agent in Texas. We hope the answer may be in the papers you were hired to intercept."

Brazos put his glass down abruptly. "I haven't been paid yet. Remember?"

"The Spider will bring the money. England and France are working day and night in Mexico City, proposing that if Mexico will recognize Texas' independence and quit plans for an invasion, they will give Texas enough financial help to keep us out of the Union. But Mexico is so damned slow."

"She is still the raped and resentful one."

"Mexico says if we are annexed she will consider it an act of war by the United States. A deadlock everywhere."

"Meantime," said Brazos, eying his cleaned plate, "Texas starves."

Trakken shrugged. "All new republics are hungry in their early years."

"Imagine it, Trakken!" He slapped both open palms upon the table. "This big country, a free Republic for eight years, now so plain belly hungry for a bone from anybody's hand that some are ready to give up! Willing to fly any damned flag if they'll send with it a shipload of flour and gold."

Trakken, studying him, said thoughtfully, "That's a thing that has always burned you deep, hasn't it? Nearly as deep as—that other business—about your father—"

Brazos spoke coldly. "I don't know how Texas will turn out. But if you will pay me my dirty damn thousand dollars, I'll soon settle the question of Seale McCloud. When I do, I can promise you somebody's blood is going to run."

He felt feverish again. Was Trakken baiting him? How much did he know about this sallow-faced man, after all? Or about Captain Spide? Saloon acquaintances, that was all: acquaintances who turned out to have a secret buyer for documents and supposedly money enough to pay him for getting them. He said, after a silence, "Is the Spider late? What time has he usually come here looking for me? I haven't got all night."

Trakken shrugged and resumed the earlier subject. "We think President Tyler will make a new proposition to Sam Houston, and England wants to know what it is. Their secret agents will pay, all right. The Spider's got it lined up. We can work all sides of this thing, McCloud. We must stay friends and trust one another." Trakken made a tired smile. "Now —about the loot?"

Brazos stared down at the sediment in the glass and saw the dregs of his father's hopes. "Poor, bastard Texas," he murmured. "Every country's slept with her. If there ever was a nameless breed, we are it." He stood. "Oh, well. We shall see. Spain's once. Yesterday, Mexico's. Today, we try it ourselves, an independent republic. Tomorrow, the highest bidder's. The poor girl in the side street off the plaza is not the only *puta* in the land having a baby tonight. At the moment, I believe we have an unfinished financial transaction to settle. You were the one who closed the deal. I look to you for the money. Now you say the Spider is to bring it. This is not smelling so good, my friend."

Trakken said silkily, "The papers? You have them?"

"Not exactly. But they're here. A whole raft of official documents. In San Antonio."

"Why didn't you bring the pouch here?"

Brazos eyed him levelly. "Because it would be cheaper to float my body down the Medina River, once the pouch is in hand."

"For God's sake, nobody's trying to do you out of your money! What makes you so suspicious?"

Brazos gave the other man a stare that caused Trakken to shift nervously. "Because it's time for the McClouds to be suspicious. I saw with my own eyes my father being marched off to Mexico in chains." He guessed he was still a little feverish. "When the money is paid to me, I'll find my father if he's been traded into Indian captivity. And I'll find the men who betrayed him."

Trakken raised one brow. "Just you against all that?"

"Not just me. You haven't met all the McClouds yet."

After a time, Trakken tried again, but half-heartedly. "You could tell me where you hid the damned government pouch."

"No," Brazos said drowsily. "I'll wait till the third member of our dirty little conspiracy shows up. Captain Spide and my thousand dollars. Or no papers."

They lapsed into a strained silence and waited for Captain Spide. Half-dozing, Brazos found himself musing upon the question of how far a man could trust a girl like Risa Driscoll. For all he knew she had already reported him to the militia. In all his years he had not met such a mixture before. Spanish coloring, dusky blue eyes, and a British accent, all in an enticing soft package, a girl who would blandly say to a strange man not much past her own age that a street woman was having a baby. But, of course, she was a doctor's daughter, and that would account for her frankness.

What if the girl chanced to look under the mattress?

What if she did that? And notified the colonel at the stockade? No, he would not let himself imagine that. He thought, instead, of how sparsely they had fed him. There was downright poverty in the Driscolls' house.

But hard times were everywhere, sparing none. The Texas Republic was in its eighth struggling year, desperately mired in the many troubles of its wobbly independence. This was 1844, and there was increasing talk that Texas must join the Union in sheer desperation. San Antonio, Brazos reflected, was the frontier town that had seen so much bloodshed and had a reason to keep one eye open at night. Every third man, some bitterly claimed, was a spy, ready to sell out to agents of the United States or Mexico, England or France.

At twenty-six, Brazos himself was a hard and wary product of the uneasy frontier. His problems had been simpler to deal with, he thought, out in the familiar dangers of the brush and prairies than in the complicated ways of town people. He studied Trakken across the room through nearly closed eyes, and murmured, "Maybe he's not coming tonight."

Trakken remarked, "Did I hear the plaza fire gong, a while back?"

"You did," Brazos replied. "I heard the sound of it, even above your oratory." He grinned. "Does the Spider like to go to a fire? Or does he find excitement enough running his hide wagons north to the Indian settlements? What's his exact business anyhow? Buffalo hides or espionage?"

There came a vigorous knocking at the door. Brazos stood and planted his back against a wall. Trakken said nervously, "Here he is. You can ask him yourself."

II

Captain Spide stepped in from the night, bringing with him the faint odor of raw buffalo hides. The hairy bullnecked man, with a smothering black beard, jerked a nod to Trakken and placed his rifle and flat-crowned hat on the table. He wasted no breath in small talk.

"Did you get what we sent you after?" The small probing eyes in his hairy face seemed to pin Brazos to the wall.

"I got it."

"Good! We picked the right man." His stocky torso made a heavy turn to Trakken. "Didn't I tell you that McCloud had the savvy for the job? Well, where is it?"

"It's here," Brazos said. "In San Antonio. Where's my money?"

Brazos saw the Spider shoot him a quick look, then twist his heavy shoulders for a digging glance at Trakken.

"He won't say." Trakken turned his palms out. "He's been at a doctor's house."

"Speak English, Trakken. He's got it or he hasn't. Which?"

An unreasonable resentment at this burned Brazos. "Do your talking with me, Captain Spide." He nodded at Trakken. "He doesn't know anything. I'm the man you're dealing with. The government pouch is in a safe place. I carried out my part of the deal and took an Indian arrow in the bargain. Now I'll have my pay."

Captain Spide spoke thickly. "You're a hotheaded fellow, McCloud. I guess we're all a little excited about this job. Now let's talk sense. We'll have the papers first. You put the documents in my hands and I'll put the money in yours."

Brazos smiled. The wine had alerted him, and he felt that a fine double cross was in the making here. "You'll have it when you get it. That will be after I see some gold."

The Spider turned his back and stalked to a chair. "Don't get mean, McCloud. We gave you a job to do. All I want to know is that you can deliver. Sit down, gentlemen. Haven't we got problems enough in this without falling out among ourselves?" The Spider smiled thinly in his beard. "Nobody else in San Antonio trusts one another. Can't we three be happy exceptions?"

Trakken sat nervously. Brazos braced against the wall again. "You go right ahead and be happy, Spider. I haven't got time. I've still got a job to do."

"I understand. You are dead set, I take it, on making the trip to Torrey's Post like you told us. That's a dangerous idea, my young friend. But I can understand what pushes you if you think your father is a captive out there. Will you tackle it alone?"

Brazos replied evasively, "My brothers will be along. Maybe others."

Trakken put in, "Don't forget, McCloud, who it is that makes it possible for you to try that."

Brazos murmured a mocking, "Thank you," but the Spider waved a thick arm and said carelessly, "Oh, don't make him feel obligations, Trakken. He's intelligent—he knows that what we pay him a thousand dollars for we have a customer who buys it from us at a profit. Simple business transaction. If the rest of Texas must starve, at least we three can avoid doing so. Now, you came here from a doctor's house, Trakken said. Would that have been Dr. Driscoll?"

"It was."

The Spider fitted his hairy fingers together. "Where the fire was."

Brazos stiffened. "What fire?"

"This evening."

"But I just came from there! Only two hours or so ago!"

"The soldiers barely missed you, then. A bucket brigade put out the flames, so I heard at the plaza just now. The soldiers were looking for a certain man. They got into an argument with a young lady. Somehow in the ruckus the lamp was upset and they soon had themselves a first-class fire on their hands. I assume the soldiers had warm ideas about the doctor's daughter, but things got hotter than they intended."

"Did they say—did you hear what room the fire was in?"

"For God's sake!" Trakken smacked the table top in exasperation. "Who cares about what room? Let's get the pouch business settled! Did you bring the money, Captain?"

The Spider watched Brazos and did not reply. Brazos said, "You two stay put a little while. I'll be back." He edged toward the door, fearful for the safety of the documents.

"Not just yet." A pistol appeared in the Spider's fist. "We'll have a bottle of your wine, Trakken, and we'll discuss this thing like good friends. Good friends, united in a great cause. Sit down, McCloud."

Reluctantly, Brazos returned to the table, seeing no way out of this delay, and no danger, either. They were not going to throw any bullets as long as they didn't know where the pouch was.

The Spider spoke. "They took that girl down to the stockade and locked her up. Then they found the doctor and locked him up, too."

Brazos moistened his lips. "Why would they do that? Just over a fire?"

The Spider chuckled. "This was a different kind of fire the doctor was playing with. He's a sympathizer, they think—been acting as a go-between with Mexico in selling Texas captives to the Indians."

"I doubt that. San Antonio is crawling with as many spies as lice, if you listen to rumors."

"He could have been the one, eh, McCloud, that handled the delivery of your father to the Comanches?"

Brazos held his eyes hard on the Spider. "Are you trying to tell me something?"

"You must be the one who was unloaded from a settler's wagon at the doctor's house. I heard a few things late today, about that." The hairy hand raised the gun. "When things quiet down a little, we'll go over there. You can show us *just where in Driscoll's house you hid the government loot.*"

The Spider was no fool. The man had sat there and all but read his mind.

"My gun," Brazos said, not moving his hand, "is one of the new Colt Paterson five-shooters. I bought it off a Ranger. If you missed me the first time, there would be two and a half bullets apiece for you and Trakken. Wouldn't a corpse feel foolish, Spider, dead from half a bullet?"

Trakken said, "Damn you, Spider, put up that thing!"

The Spider hesitated, then reluctantly returned his gun to his belt. "I heard a new rumor on the plaza today, McCloud."

It could be bait and probably was. Yet Brazos could not refrain from jumping at it. Hoarsely, he asked, "My father?"

"Came pretty straight, from Bartolo himself. Some specific names of the captives up there and how they may be ransomed."

Brazos felt his mouth turn dry. "Go ahead."

"They were brought up from Mexico City. From Perote Prison. The Mexicans turned them over to the Comanches.

Some had been captured on the Santa Fe expedition, some from the time Woll's army retreated out of here. Maybe one is your father." The Spider laced his hirsute fingers and studied them.

"You know the only name I'm interested in! Was Seale McCloud mentioned?"

The Spider glanced at Trakken and their eyes held for a moment. Without turning, he said, "Just bring the documents to me, McCloud. That will help me to remember."

"I'll want the money. And what you heard from Bartolo."

"That's understood. You feel like making the walk, McCloud?"

"I feel like it. Just don't coyote after me. You'll see me when you see me."

"Tonight?"

"Tomorrow would serve better." There would be less chance of a pistol going off if they were on the plaza in daylight. "Watch in the street across from Mealey's. When you see me, follow me. Have the money in a bag of some kind, in your hand."

"We understand each other." The Spider gestured benevolently.

At the door, Brazos murmured, "I hope we do. Good night."

The walk back through the blackness seemed twice as long as before and his muscles twice as reedy. The starlit world dipped a little under his feet. A throb returned to his shoulder wound. Somewhere toward the plaza in the center of the darkened settlement he caught sounds of a running horse and the barking of a dog pack. He emerged from the brush at the road and sighted the Driscoll house, a squat chunk of shadow. He sniffed the odor of smoke and charred wood. Something moved, and he made out the sentry leaning against an oak tree in the yard.

Approaching him, Brazos saw the militiaman shift erect and peer against the darkness.

"This where the fire was?" Brazos asked.

"Yeah."

"Do much damage?"

"Not much. Them walls're mud, they don't burn. Lot of excitement, though, for a few minutes."

"Where're the people who live here?"

"They got 'em down at the stockade. Mexican spies, I heard. They put me on watch here, for no reason that makes sense to me. Mind to walk off and leave it. Would, if they didn't owe me three months' back pay. What uh army!"

"Yes, what an army," Brazos said sympathetically. "Do you have the sentry duty all to yourself, or is there somebody at the back?"

"Myself. You know where a feller might could get a job?"

Brazos chuckled. "A job in Texas?"

"I know," the other said forlornly. "It's hell, ain't it?"

"Well, time for me to be getting home. *Buenas noches.*"

Brazos headed for the road, walked east a quarter of a mile, and then doubled back. He noiselessly approached the Driscoll house from the rear and found the back door unlocked. In another minute he was fumbling under the stuffed bed ticking where he had come back to consciousness. The smell of smoke and scorched flooring still lay heavy, but a greater heaviness caught him in his chest when his hand failed to touch the soft leather of the government pouch. Carefully, he felt along the space between slats and mattress on one side, and then on the other, and went to his stomach to run his hands over every inch of the floor underneath. The pouch was not there.

He searched over the room as best he could in the darkness, knowing this was futile. Then he heard voices in the yard at the front. Probably the sentry's relief had come.

He hesitated, wondering where he might go to spend the rest of the night. He decided against waking his uncle, Moss Dean, and anyhow that would be a long walk. He felt a great tiredness. Quickly, he rolled a blanket from the bed and slipped soundlessly from the rear door. In a little while he was bedded down in a brushy clump on a singing bend of the river, closing his eyes to uneasy sleep.

III

The Plaza de las Yslas stirred to another sultry dawn.

San Antonio de Bexar came lazily awake and here in the broad cobblestone middle of the town the first life moved in a new day. Yesterday had been all famine of food and feast of rumors. Today would be no different.

The plaza began to stretch to the scented heaviness of pig puddles, old jasmine blooms, mule rigging, and the sour-sweet remnants of last night's saloon trade. Eastward lay the emptiness of Yturri Street, its white dust not yet raised by the army patrol that soon would ride off to circle the country for Indian signs.

On the south side, where the Military Plaza linked onto the larger Yslas, the cottonwoods drooped foliage made sickly by the rancid smoke of the army blacksmith forges. The area was disfigured by the run-down straggle of stone fences and walls surrounding the prison, the military barracks, and Council House.

The first raggedy drifters, white, brown, and mixed, padded into the plaza. A man drank at the well in front of the Council House and told his listeners, between draughts, that the woman in Noche Alley had had her baby last night, in good shape, a blue-eyed Mexican boy. A philosopher in rags, following the other at the bucket, commented, "What's one more bastard in this country?"

"Aye," said another, "we'll all end belonging to Mexico again, and that'll make him legitimate."

Also, it was recounted that the volunteer brigade had performed ably, if tardily, at the fire in the house of the new doctor.

"The *bastardo* was a spy for Santa Anna," said an old Mexican, a town native even before the Anglos came.

"No, it was his daughter."

"Every other candle across town lights the house of a spy, to hear the militia tell it."

The man at the well finished his toilet by dipping his gnarled hands into the wooden bucket and then rubbing his whiskers. "Not enough rations to feed the soldiers, much less all the spy suspects they catch."

"But this doctor is a bad one. I heard it straight from a soldier. He was harboring a wounded man, some outlaw trying to escape to Salido. The Mexicans have got their men everywhere. I look for another invasion, just any sunup."

"He heard it straight," mimicked a black-shawled old woman. "Every lie that was ever told, the *soldado* heard it straight." She hoisted her bundle of sticks and drifted on.

Brazos McCloud waited at a shadowy corner near the entrance to the stockade. A militia officer turned the corner. He wore patched walnut cottonspun and the homemade shoulder straps of a captain.

"A minute, Captain!" Brazos stepped into his path. "Can you tell me anything about the doctor and his daughter who were arrested last night? My wife is having a baby. I need to find Dr. Driscoll."

"Good Godamighty!" The captain twisted his palms out, almost angrily. "Whatta you want that *espia* deliverin' 'er for? Get Doc Jenkins."

"I need help. Her time's come, we think."

"Driscoll is pullin' out of town soon as we can load him up. The colonel is givin' him and his gal till noon to haul freight."

"And why is that?"

"A spy, I tell you! For the City of Mexico."

The captain gestured a so-long and turned for the doorway. Brazos caught his sleeve. "If I could just see Driscoll for a minute—just to tell him the symptoms, how it is this morning."

The captain softened. "All right, come on!" Brazos followed him through the dingy patio toward a distant iron door. Beyond that the captain directed a jailor to unlock another door, and then Brazos stood in a small room where he saw the dim outlines of the two prisoners.

"This man's havin' calvin' trouble," the captain grunted. Brazos saw Driscoll unfold to his feet and peer hard at him, and he saw his flicker of recognition.

"About my wife, Doctor." He winked wildly. Driscoll stared hard and mumbled. Brazos turned to the captain. "This is kind of personal. About my wife, you know."

"Don't mind me, friend. I've seen bornin's from start to finish."

"But there's a girl here."

The captain grunted and walked out of the room. When the door closed, Brazos caught Driscoll by the arm and brought his mouth close to the man's ear. "Those papers, damn you! Where are they?"

"Papers?"

"The pouch I left under your mattress. What did you do with it?"

Driscoll twisted and tried to penetrate the gloom in a hostile upward stare at Brazos. Risa Driscoll's voice came coldly from the across the cell. "He doesn't know anything about your papers."

He whirled to her. "Then you do!"

"Perhaps I do."

"Where are they?"

She was silent and he felt desperation clutching his insides. "Would pay interest you?"

"It might. Gold?"

"Gold. What is your price?"

"What's this about, daughter?"

"Quiet, father. We're penniless and we need money to travel on. There's an opportunity here."

Brazos said, "This is very important to me. There's a man's life at stake in this."

"You started all our troubles," she said aloofly. "The soldiers were looking for you. They claim we harbored a spy."

"Please, miss, everything in Texas is mixed up. This is life or death. Where is my pouch?"

"If the documents are valuable," Risa said hesitantly, "then I would guess they were *stolen* papers. Ah, your expression confirms that. So I think I shall just know to myself what I know. We're in trouble. Perhaps I have something now to bargain with. Gold will talk."

Brazos wanted to seize her and shake the truth out of her. A fist pounded the door. "Hey, come on, now—you've had long enough in there!"

Imploringly, Brazos whispered to the girl: "Where will you go from here? Where will I find you? I'll pay!"

"We have nowhere to go," she replied simply. "You wish to suggest a place?"

He said urgently, "Then go to my home—the McCloud place. My family will put you up. Tell them Brazos sent you —go there, and wait. Take the pouch. Will you do that? I'll pay your price."

Dr. Driscoll grumbled, "I don't understand this."

She murmured aloofly: "Perhaps we will. We must go *somewhere*."

Hurriedly, he whispered the directions, explaining the route as best he could, not sure that they understood, not even sure that they would accept his suggestion. The captain was calling and urging him to come along. Brazos thanked the captain for his help and emerged to the plaza walk. The captain was looking at him oddly, as if trying to remember. Brazos began the angle across the open cobblestones of the plaza.

From the tail of his eye he caught the sudden reappearance of the captain in the doorway. Sleep was dying in the captain's brain. Maybe he was belatedly remembering a description. Brazos increased his pace.

A backward glance showed him that the captain had now come to the edge of the walk and was staring after him.

Then the captain whistled shrilly. Brazos ignored this and walked faster. The loungers across the way at the well were taking it in. The captain started walking hurriedly after him. Brazos began a slow jog. The skinny captain went into a trot, too.

The man's yell shrilled down the block. "Hey, *McCloud!*"

Brazos fogged through the tangle of wagons, carts, and Mexican peddlers, dodged into the first alley and turned on a full run. He sloshed through a mud puddle, hurdled a dozing sow, sped into a weedy patio and swung over a low stone fence. His wound throbbed, and he was afraid the bleeding had started again. He sprinted for the next alley. When that opened upon a vacant stretch of broomweeds, he dodged back to the scattering of houses at his left, cut across a narrow street, walked through the Lone Star Saloon, out the rear and hurried down Crockett Street. He turned the corner, stopped, and peered back, showing only one eye and his hat brim. The captain pounded out of an alleyway two blocks distant. Brazos, with a curse for the persistent trooper, broke into a run. In midblock, before the captain had time to round the corner, he stopped before the door of a log house. Overhead a charcoal-lettered sign said: MOSS DEAN. SADDLER.

Brazos whipped inside and dropped the bolt lock in place. Sunlight bathed the interior from windows opening to a patio at the rear. The black whiskered face of a stooped giant turned to scowl at him. A big hand paused with round knife suspended over a half-finished saddle fender.

"Somebody after you?"

"Right behind me, Uncle Moss."

"Put an apron on. Keep your back turned." The big man moved swiftly for his size as he tossed Brazos an apron. Brazos tied it on and concealed his hat behind a barrel of leather scraps.

"Work at that bench there. Don't turn around."

Brazos faced a saddler's bench. He caught up a wood bouncer and began to rub down the cut leather of a saddle seat. "This look all right?"

"Easy there!" the big man warned. "You'll waste a good hide."

"Better this than my own."

Boots thudded outside. The door bar rattled, a fist banged. "Hey, in there! Open up! Army!"

Moss negligently plodded to the door, took his time opening it, and blocked the space with his bulk. The hard-puffing captain tried to push past him. "A man run in here a minute ago, Dean?"

"Through a locked door, Myrick?"

"Out of my way, man!"

Moss let the puffing, red-bearded soldier squeeze past. The captain had lost his hat in the chase. He took a quick look around the leather-smelly room. Moss asked, "What're you chasin'?"

"Fellow I think's named McCloud."

Sparing only a negligent look at the man whose head was bent to his work at the bench, the captain opened the back door, looked into the yard, and whirled back to the front. He was almost to the street door, where Moss waited with his hand on the knob, when Brazos with a sickening knowledge heard the boots skid to a halt. He knew that the officer was coming back to circle for a close look at his face. His hand tightened on the wood bouncer and he slowed his strokes against the seat leather.

Now the captain stood almost at his left elbow, craning around to see. The triumphant grunt of recognition had just formed in his throat when Brazos aimed by instinct and swung with the fist bouncer. The hard crashing smack of wood against the bare skull sent the militiaman sagging into an unconscious heap on the floor.

Moss looked down at the crumpled form. "I believe what Wid said, they should have named you Trouble, whether there was such a river or not. Red Myrick's all right—I could have talked him out of—"

Brazos demanded, "What's the report on me?"

"Last night at Mealey's they had it that some fellow here in Bexar was wanted on a complaint out of Austin. He robbed a Union diplomatic courier."

"How'd they know that?"

"Word of it got to the American consul at Austin," his uncle replied. "The government sicked the militia and Rangers both to find the bandit. Some homesteaders talked in the plaza after dumping a wounded man at Doc Driscoll's three or four days ago. Now I'm adding it up. Why didn't you cover your mug when you did it?"

"I was wrapped like a mummy!"

"You wasn't wrapped enough. A feller on the stage thought he recognized the man from hanging around Mealey's. Referred to him as the one that always made strong talk against annexation." Brazos saw Moss's shaggy features crinkle. Moss said, "It ain't for the Union they want you most. Sam Houston slipped the word to Colonel Davis that he'd like to have a private look at them papers you stole, hisself. Before anybody else."

Brazos had considered that. But no matter if circumstances had given him something that would be useful to the Republic, perhaps even new, strong cards in the present critical bargaining over annexation, his father was still a prisoner. He had to have the thousand dollars.

Moss Dean's rough voice softened. "I guess it has to do with the ransom." He jerked a thumb to indicate a far place north. "Up there."

"Torrey's Post. Yes. It's still like we planned, Moss, if I get my pay."

"You still figure Seale's up yonder?"

"The Mexicans passed about twenty captives on to the Indians. Some from the Woll raid, some from the Santa Fe and Mier expeditions. That's how Santa Anna buys Indian support. This came from Bartolo himself."

"By what route?"

"The Spider and Trakken. The Spider got it from a Cherokee on the prairie, and the Indian had the word from Bartolo. We can get him back, Moss!" His voice grew husky with a mixture of hope and challenge. Just the dim promise of success, after such a long time, made his blood pound. "The Mexican agents are doing it that way to prod the Comanches to keep raiding. You know how Mexico is trying to stir up the tribes against us. We can buy him back, if we have the price. God, what I might do if I had that thousand dollars!"

Moss frowned. "You meanin' you pulled that job on credit? Who for?"

"Captain Spide and Trakken. They're selling the documents to England, so they claim. That was my mistake, the credit was." He moved about nervously in the small open space, watching the captain's still form. "But he'll pay. He and Trakken have a buyer. Trouble is, the damn documents have disappeared."

The captain groaned, squirmed a little, then lay still again.

"Don't worry about him," Moss said. "He won't like the way you dehorned him, but he's a man that can be trusted once he knows what's up. Go on—tell me what's next."

IV

Everything had gone wrong. He hurt inwardly at the disgrace of having to relate this to Wid and Teche. Here he was struggling to escape the town but with one foot caught, the trap being his compulsion to finish his deal with the Spider and Trakken. Yet flight appeared imperative, else he soon would be a prisoner in the stockade and he would never find the papers.

He said, "There's a hill somewhere that needs me behind it, Uncle Moss. Can you handle this trouble if I take out?"

"I will. Don't you boys start till I get there." Moss's voice turned worried. "One thing. You ever considered that the pair you hired to might be workin' for Mexico?"

"Of course. There was always that possibility." Brazos frowned. Couldn't his uncle see that only the money counted? "What difference would that make? To a man held in some Indian camp?"

"Don't rear up at me, but it would make a difference. Knowin' Seale like I do, he wouldn't want it that way."

Hotly Brazos refused to accept that. With his jaw tense he told Moss, "I'm heading to Torrey's Post with the money on me, when I get it. Wid and Teche will be along. Anybody who tries to block us have invited themselves to a contest."

"You McClouds! All right, count me, too. I'll be ridin' with you."

"You don't have to, Moss."

"Yeah, I have to. I wouldn't want Seale to think I was safe here whittlin' saddles while his boys needed me. The officials have all turned against him on account of that treason talk. His enemies at Austin played free and fancy with that gossip because Seale was mighty powerful on the side of those against annexation!"

The captain kicked to a sitting position and opened his eyes.

"If Wid ever knows you did this to Red Myrick, he'll skin you both alive."

Brazos and Moss exchanged curious glances. "Do you know Wid?" Brazos demanded.

"How do you think it dawned on me you was a McCloud? You're alike as two live oaks. Now help me up. My head's bustin'."

"Prove what you say."

"I will. You're Brazos McCloud and there's one between you and Wid named Teche, and two girls younger, Sabine and Neches. Moss Dean here is your uncle. I side-kicked with Wid in Old Paint Caldwell's battalion. Wid's leg is off at the right knee, and Red Myrick's the one who carried him back to the Salado after he caught the cannon burst, and he bloodied us both aplenty."

Brazos reached to help the man stand. The captain had left no doubt, but he was not through yet. "If you want to know what Wid said then, he said, 'If I die I don't want to carry a messy pulp like that to glory, so go on and cut it off.' It finally hit me you was a McCloud and I chased you because I wanted to tell you something you ought to know. You're a McCloud all right. You slug me first and ask questions later."

Moss dampened a rag at the water bucket and dabbed at the knot swelling from Myrick's pinkish hair. Then he handed the captain a bottle of rye whisky. Brazos voiced an apology and waited.

"I've heard what you've been sayin'," Myrick mumbled, when he got his breathing under control. "You're the holdup man, all right. Listen, I'm goin' to Torrey's Post with you. Wid will tell you I'd be a good man to have along. The reason is, I've got a brother who's a captive, too. From the Mier expedition. Never heard hide nor hair, till lately, then word came they might have traded him up from Mexico City."

"What was it important you wanted to tell me?"

"There's a description out for you," Myrick explained, "but not by name. Colonel Davis sent soldiers last night to look at a wounded man some homesteaders dropped off at Doc Driscoll's. Homesteaders put it out that the man was right fond of a government-looking pouch, even when he was unconscious. The Rangers are being sent to get you and some kind of papers you're supposed to have. The colonel got the impression you pulled it for our government. Did you? You pull this thing for Sam Houston?"

He did not know how much he should tell Myrick. But there was an opportunity here to get the militia pressure off his neck. He seized it.

"Suppose you tell Davis to forget about me. Sam Houston will not want me hounded by the militia. He won't like having me hamstrung by Davis' garrison. This is confidential."

Red Myrick looked suspiciously at Brazos. "Somehow, I doubt if this is so, but I'll swear to the truth of it."

"Just tell your commander to leave me free to maneuver, else he's likely to hear directly from Sam Houston in a way that will curl his shoulder straps off his uniform."

Myrick held his head and managed to part his pinkish beard in a painful smile. "I'll tell the colonel when I turn in my resignation. That won't be no longer than fifteen minutes from now. When do we start for Comanche country?"

"You're sure itchin', Red," Moss commented.

"Well, you know of any better time than today? I'm one that likes to get started. The army's not payin' us anything but paper scrip, down to a nickel on the dollar. Ain't you heard Texas is tryin' to borrow money all over the world? The rations don't make it worth while, either. A man can resign and walk off if he wants to, all they ask you to do is grab a gun and hurry back if the Mexicans invade."

Brazos felt a growing liking for Red Myrick. He visualized his act of carrying the wounded Wid out of the battle on the Salado.

"Suppose you go settle things with the colonel, Myrick. Put it out that I'm working for the Texas government. Then—"

"Of course that story will fizzle soon as the Rangers get here from Austin," Myrick put in.

"I hope to be a far piece gone by then. First, I need to have a talk with a pair named Trakken and Captain Spide. You know them?"

"I know who you mean. Spide runs the hide wagons north. Trakken's a land agent or somethin'. They hang around Mealey's, talkin' for England."

"Right. Then, if you want to ride north with us, you and Moss and I will go to our place, which is a long day south. I want Wid and Teche in on what we do from there on. First thing as I see it, is to find the Driscolls."

Moss said he could manage for three mustangs. "We'll also need supplies. I've got frijoles and corn meal, and a few things. Short on ammunition." He squinted at the captain. "Any ideas, Red?"

"I can get off with a little ammunition, if they don't watch me too close." Then Red asked, grinning, "What about the baby your wife is about to have? Were you takin' me in?"

Brazos matched his grin. "We called the whole thing off." At the doorway he said, "See you at Mealey's. If I'm in close talk with the Spider and Trakken, don't crowd us. It's just as well they don't know we're together in this. But keep your eyes open."

Brazos walked toward the plaza with McCloud violins
playing inside. His little sister, Neches, must have had a
good dream last night. He went to a back table in the mid-
morning gloom of Mealey's scrubbed-wood shadows. He
took a chair, running a quick study over the sprinkling of
customers. One man at the bar he knew, but Brazos nodded
aloofly and the man kept his place. The others he dismissed
as nondescript morning patrons. All except one.

This man was a stranger to him. He, too, sat alone at a
table, toying with a whisky. His hatchet-shaped profile was
poorly outlined in the shadows. Brazos felt quick distrust
of the man's stoop-shouldered, furtive appearance.

The bartender raised an eyebrow from behind the counter
and Brazos nodded. When the small brandy came the bar-
keep spoke from the corner of his mouth. "Dirty weather
we're havin'."

"Squall, you think?"

"Might be. Cloudin' up."

"Thanks, Mike."

Brazos raised the glass and studied with new concern in
the movement the lone man across the room. What was
Mike trying to tell him? That yonder was a bad one?

He waited out a dragging hour. He dismissed as quickly
as he could the few saloon acquaintances who came over to
speak with him. The hatchet-faced man waited, too, and
none came to his table.

The time neared noon and trade picked up. Still, he had not
sighted either set of his conspirators through the window facing the plaza. He waited with growing uneasiness, and hoped
that no militiaman would look in before Red Myrick spread
the story that Brazos McCloud was a government agent for
Sam Houston and not to be molested.

The next pair of clattering boots through the doorway belonged to Moss Dean and Red Myrick. They paused as
Brazo sighted them, then turned for the bar when he
shook his head. Almost at the same time, he caught a glimpse
of Trakken and the Spider across the plaza. Business was
coming to a head all of a sudden. He arose and walked toward the doorway.

He passed behind the backs of Moss and Red, not speaking, but seeing their eyes tail him in the mirror. The hatchet-
faced man behind the table at the left wall had his head down
but his hat brim turned. The bartender said something in an
undertone to Moss.

From the walk, Brazos found the pair again, the squat dark figure and the bent taller one, in the shadows on the other side. Wagon and saddlehorse movement mixed between, a slow coming and going.

They sighted him almost at once. Brazos noted, with quickening blood beat, that the Spider carried a bag in his hairy fist.

Something flagged his attention from behind, causing him to cut his head the cautious inch that gave him eye-tail sight of the saloon glass at his back. A foggy figure floated there, enough of him visible to show the hatchet-faced man. He had come near the window. Brazos also spied the outlines of Moss and Red drifting toward the doorway.

He sauntered out of sight of Mealey's window to the corner of the walk and made a signal to the Spider and Trakken, indicating the side alley. He walked down the weedy tracks and waited at the rear corner of the building. One of Mealey's back rooms would be empty at this hour. It was his purpose to take them there. When the two came in sight, he pointed, then ducked around to Mealey's back door. He waited until Trakken and the Spider turned the corner.

"This will be private, in here." He opened the door.

Then he caught a glimpse of movement within the dark passageway. The shadow moved from the saloon's inner door: the low-holstered gun, the pulled-down hat, the thin figure of the hatchet-faced man.

"Not here," the Spider mumbled behind Brazos. "We have a better place." He turned away.

Brazos tagged them down the alley, the gold in the bag like a bait that led him on behind them. They passed through a grove of trees and turned toward the dust-shrouded cattle pens. The Spider and Trakken disappeared into a work shack adjacent to the pens. The dusty air was filled with the din of loud-bawling longhorns. Brazos followed and Trakken closed the door. The Spider smacked the bag on a table, but kept his fist tightened to the twist of the canvas.

"One thousand in gold. *Mucho dinero*, these days."

Trakken fidgeted, and Brazos remarked the sweat on his sallow face. The man was uncommonly nervous. Captain Spide searched Brazos with his darting black eyes.

"Show us something, McCloud. Let's see what you've brought."

Brazos felt a dislike for the setting, for the feeling he was having about this, for the hatchet-faced man who had worried out the time with him in Mealey's.

"Fact is," Brazos smiled disarmingly, "when I went to get the loot, it had been moved. But have no fear," he added hastily, "it only delays the matter a few days."

He might have loosed a rattlesnake in the room. He could hear Trakken's fast breathing, the Spider's unintelligible mutter rumbling up. "I know where the pouch is," Brazos went on, as if this were a small thing. "I would like to ask," he said, deciding to be brazen, "if you will pay me now? Trust me for delivery. It will make a difference, I assure you. I will give you my word not to fail you."

The two turned their attention from him, looked questioningly at each other, and Trakken made a nervous gesture.

"It is too big a risk to take."

The Spider mumbled, "How many days, McCloud?"

"No more than two or three, I would hope. Maybe sooner."

He heard the footstep outside the door. In the same instant, the hairy one clutched the money sack more tightly against his stomach. The door inched open.

The hatchet-faced man walked in. His gun was in his hand.

Trakken coughed with a choking sound and the Spider shook his head.

The hatchet-face made a crazy slit of a smile. "I'll take that bag off you."

"What is this?" Brazos demanded.

Then he saw the man's eyes turn glassy mean and the pale face convulse. The man's white finger fitted itself to the trigger. Brazos' brain shrilled the double cross, and murder —revealed now and ugly, and only an eyewink away.

"I'll take that bag of money," the man said again.

As if nobody else understood and this thing needed a label on it, Trakken brightly croaked, "It's a robbery!" His voice cracked.

Moss Dean and Red Myrick slid through the doorway with guns out. The man turned, and Moss, who was ahead of Red, saw the gun and acted without a break in his stride. He slapped his pistol across the man's ear. The man stumbled, fell, and lay still.

Brazos whirled back to keep his Colt trained on the Spider and Trakken. Their plot to kill him, or at least to rob him of his new-paid money, lay bare in the room like a stretched hide for all to look at.

"Your man wasn't rehearsed enough. I hadn't even got my hands on the money," he said.

"No—no!" Trakken sputtered.

"By God, McCloud, I don't know a thing about this!" the Spider protested. "If you're saying I framed something, you're making dangerous talk."

"That's what I'm saying."

Brazos reached abruptly for the moneybag. To hell with waiting. He held his gun on the Spider and pulled the heavy sack across the table. "I'm taking this while the taking's good. I'll send the papers, like I agreed to."

"Don't be so honest!" Moss retorted. "They was goin' to rob you."

Brazos moved back a pace. "I owe them the documents. You'll get them, Spider."

The Spider's brushy eyes glowed with red malice. "Thief!"

"Well, now, we're men of honor, Captain Spide. You said so, yourself. I'll take my money now, and you'll get the loot. That will make us honest, all around."

Trakken crushed his knuckles. "I didn't know a thing about this."

"If you can hush this up, Captain Spide, you'll save us all from bad trouble. He was your man." Brazos motioned to the unconscious form on the floor.

"I'll expect those papers," the Spider muttered.

"You have my word. Somehow, Captain, I have had the feeling all along that when I got my money from you it would have to be at the point of a gun."

Red said, "Let's get out of here."

They cut across to the alley at a jog. Brazos asked, "Where to?"

"We'd better lay low at Red's today," Moss replied. "We got some outfittin' to do."

Brazos knew a weakness again in his legs, and the good tinkle of gold coins, and the thin margin by which he was alive. "Laying low suits me, too," he said. "I'm still a little shy of blood, I think." The gold was in his hands, though, and it was better than blood.

V

Wid McCloud, the oldest of the clan, was the only one not named for a stream. The crossings of the rivers westward had not yet begun when Wid was born. He was a stocky, long-haired man of thirty, whose ordeal of pain had shadowed his eyes and cut age crevices into his jaw. Once in a saddle he was secure; it was getting there that took doing. The action at San Jacinto had left their father, Seale McCloud, and their uncle, Moss Dean, unscathed. But the later battle with Woll's Mexican invaders had cost Seale's oldest son a leg, and Wid lived with a continuous pain in his knee stump.

This morning, he was the last to be seated at the table in the low-ceilinged kitchen lean-to. It took a little time and patience to work his smoothly whittled walnut peg and leather knee strappings into place. Once established, he inspected the row of lowered heads.

"You, Sabine."

The girl said, "Lord bless this food. Lord keep Texas out of the Union. Lord send our father back to us safe. Amen."

Four voices repeated, "Amen."

Teche's honey-complexioned wife, the only fair-skinned one among them, said lightly, "Grits and venison again. I hope you don't mind."

Wid's lined features showed amusement. "What if we did mind, Ann? Would you secede from the McClouds and annex the Union?"

"I might," she said with mock severity, "if I could take Teche with me."

Teche, her tall, bronzed husband, did not smile. He was next to Wid in age and the only married one, and he had been hard-worked in these recent weeks with Brazos gone.

Sabine repeated her favorite joke. "We were the reason the United States Senate voted against annexation. They wouldn't take Texas if the McClouds had to be included."

"Serve them right if we sold ourselves to England," Teche remarked. "Sabine, you working cattle with me today? You keep a sharp lookout for those Cherokee boys."

Sabine, who was sixteen, exclaimed, "I'm ready to ride when you are!"

Teche said, "Lucky family. Where would you find five better ranch hands in all Texas?"

"Five?" Ann pretended a hurt. "Why not six? Don't I do my part?"

"I was counting you," Teche retorted.

Ann murmured a caution. Wid frowned. Neches, the youngest, now fourteen and who had been only eleven when Seale McCloud had disappeared, made an angry clash with her fork against her crockery plate.

"Then you're not counting Brazos!" she accused. "Shame on you, Teche!"

"I'll do my own arithmetic, baby."

Nobody said anything, and Neches' dark cheeks flushed. Ann brought the granite pot from the fireplace and filled the cups with the boiling mixture of precious coffee padded with parched acorns. Neches' face was likely to switch from thunderclouds to luminous sunshine in a matter of seconds, and it did so now. The baby of the family furnished the dreams for the breakfast table. She remembered last night's. Her abruptly excited eyes made a sweep of them all.

"I had a wonderful dream," she breathed. "The starlight came through the window. The whole world turned pink and pretty, like Ann's skin and Wid, you had your leg back. Then they released *all* the prisoners from the Perote dungeon. There was music of a hundred fiddlers at once and the mesquites began to shine like soapy water was poured over them and Father came marching home at the head of all the prisoners, laughing for us and carrying a beautiful Texas flag. And he wasn't hurt a bit!"

There was no comment for that, but the girl kept the dream in her dark eyes while the others concentrated on their food and their own thoughts. When the silence had stretched out for a time, Teche worked for the last coffee drops in his cup, pushed back from the table, and brought out pipe and tobacco.

"Maybe Neches can dream up what's become of Brazos."

"Maybe I can!" The child beamed at everyone. "I'll try to. Oh, it would be wonderful to dream that Father and Brazos both came home and we were all here together, even eating grits and jerky and old salty smelly bacon. That would be like a *thousand* fiddles singing!"

Sabine laughed outright. Wid made a deep chuckling sound. Ann patted her husband's arm. "Teche, do you want to bet me something that some day her dreams don't all come true?"

Teche kept his eyes down to the job of filling his pipe. "Why would Brazos want to come back?"

Wid's tone went ominously low. "Why wouldn't he?"

"Because working this spread is not like hanging around those Bexar saloons! If you ask me, Brazos has gone to the bad in a handbasket."

"What he's trying to do is with my approval," Wid said sternly. "All of us agreed on that. One of us had to be doing *something*—Brazos was the one to work on it, to try to find out what information he could, and San Antonio de Bexar was the place to do it. It's the duty of the rest of us to keep this place going."

"You wouldn't want Father to think we'd completely given up!" Sabine added accusingly.

"No use," Teche said doggedly. "We couldn't pay the ransom even if Brazos made a contact. Lot different, chasing longhorns in the thickets all day, from loafing around the plaza groggeries."

Wid smacked the table with a mighty fist. His wooden leg kicked the floor. "There'll be no talk like that in this house, Teche! By God, we've fought along together against everything so far, and we're going to be still hanging together as a family when it's all over."

"If Brazos doesn't hang by himself beforehand."

"Brazos is trying to do something. Whatever it is, he's one to do a thing his own way."

Teche saw the hurt expressions of his two young sisters, and the anger in Wid's cloudy eyes. "I'm sorry," he said gruffly.

Sabine stood. She was a well formed young woman, attractive in spite of her hand-me-down riding garb. Her glance narrowed at the window. "Somebody's coming. In a wagon."

Wid worked himself erect, stumped across the room, and strapped on his gun belt.

The first rim of the new sun showed across the mesquite valley as they straggled out into the baked *caliche* yard.

A spring wagon rattled past the pole corral. They saw a long-beaked man with unkempt mustache and an expression of permanent irritation. The girl on the seat beside him was dark-skinned, erect, and unsmiling, taking in the flock of McClouds with a level glance. Her slender fingers lay clasped in the lap of her loose and faded calico.

The man singled out Wid. "This the McCloud place?"

"Of course, Father," the girl said quietly. "I can see the resemblance."

Wid spoke politely. "Won't you get down?"

"We're looking for Brazos McCloud," the man said gruffly. "He about?"

"I'm his brother. Anything I can do for you?"

"I'm Doctor Driscoll. This is Risa, my daughter. We expected to find. Brazos McCloud here."

"Won't you come in, Miss Driscoll?" Ann asked. The girl turned to her father with a question.

The doctor nodded. "Get down, Risa. I'm tired of running."

She stepped to the front wheel, then to the hub, and gracefully to the ground with unconcern for the momentary high exposure of brown flesh.

Wid repeated, "Running?"

"The da—the blasted Texas army."

"Prudente, Father!"

"Burned us out, locked us up, ordered us out of town! How's that stump, man? Hurt like all of 'em do?"

"A little."

"I know. You mean plenty. San Jacinto?"

"No. My father was there. But I got this when Woll marched on San Antonio." Wid added shortly, "My father was one of the prisoners they carried off when they retreated to Mexico."

Dr. Driscoll whistled. "You folks've had it rough. Now your brother's got an arrow wound and maybe half of Texas after him. That's what put me in a pickle."

They were moving toward the doorway, the sisters and Ann shyly eying the new girl, Wid and Teche studying the doctor. Wid stopped. His gaze suddenly turned hard and unfriendly.

"Will you say that again? You talking about Brazos?"

"I am. He's in trouble with the Union law and the Republic law and no telling who else. Now they got me mixed in—claim I'm a Mexican sympathizer or something."

"Well, are you?"

"What if I was?"

"You wouldn't be welcome here!"

The doctor cocked an eyebrow. "You for annexing?"

"No. We're for staying what we fought to be—a free republic."

The girl turned to Wid and said, "Father's a born arguer.

He's not really a sympathizer. If he hadn't carried such a chip on his shoulder the militia might have listened to an explanation. It was only a happenstance that we had your brother in our house."

Teche asked, "Well, was that any crime?"

"The officials seemed to think so!" Driscoll said. "Fools! Little wonder the Republic is dying on the vine. If they haven't got any more sense at the capitol than they show at Sanantone, Mexico or England will be owning us in a matter of weeks."

They were still clustered awkwardly at the doorway. Wid said, "About Brazos. Tell it plain, mister. What's his trouble?"

Driscoll grimaced. "He's supposed to have robbed a Union messenger. Government documents. He's lost more blood than he knows. Arrow wound. And he's been keeping company wth a couple of saloon characters in town, a pair of cutthroats believed to be secret agents for England. That's a start. I can give you a full diagnosis better on a full stomach. I say, I need a shot of whisky."

"Come on in," Wid said. "Ann, would you—"

"Food in five minutes!" She headed for the fireplace.

Sabine said, "Would you like to freshen up a little—Risa?"

"Thank you. We loaded and left in a hurry. What were the names, again?"

"I'm Sabine. This is Neches. She was the last river my parents settled on, before this place."

"Pardon?"

"We're all rivers. All but Wid. They hadn't started moving around, then. Teche is not exactly a river. He's a bayou in Louisiana."

"Just a muddy bayou," Neches added. "It makes him mad."

"You all look so much alike!"

"Do you know Brazos?" Sabine asked eagerly. "Did you see the resemblance?"

Risa looked steadily at the two girls. "I don't exactly know him. But there is a resemblance. Only, he was a little whiter than the rest of you, the last time I had a good look at him."

"And when was that?"

"The time I speak of was when my father was away delivering a baby. Your brother was in a hurry to go somewhere, so fast that he mistook a window for the door."

Sabine gasped. "Brazos did that?"

"And just in time. Three soldiers came, looking for him."

"Then you had your hands full."

"That was what *they* had in mind with me, it seemed," Risa said calmly. "I never saw so many hands in all my life. It's come to a fine pass in Texas when you can save your honor only by setting your house afire. So they got even by arresting me for a spy."

Sabine's eyes glowed with admiration. "You must be stronger than you look."

"We had the Battle of San Jacinto all over again and a lamp got upset. Yes, I might say that I slightly know your brother. You will pardon my indiscretion as your guest if I also say that I don't know one thing good about him. He has caused us quite a bit of misery."

"It takes a little time," Neches said distantly, "to know us McClouds. But we're nice people."

"*Apologia!* It's just that the fools took me to the stockade, and then my father, and we've had no sleep."

Teche asked, "When they turned you loose, why did you head for this place?"

They saw Risa's hesitation. "Brazos suggested it. He left something at our house. Something that looked important enough that I felt we should find him, so that I could tell him."

The scissortail mustangs were sorry horseflesh for certain, but the best that Moss and Red could furnish. The three long-haired animals walked single file into the night. The Republic's saturating poverty, thought Brazos, hit horses first and men second, scarcity of corn and maize being what it was. But if these scissortails made it home they might be good for the hard distance north. The skinniest horse-flesh sometimes had more stamina for a hard trail than fat ones, like humans. But unless the Driscolls had followed his offer to take refuge at the McCloud ranch, he would wind up back home as empty-handed as when he had started out. He knew he could not use that gold until the documents were delivered to Trakken and the Spider. Call it conscience —it was the way it was. Wid would be disappointed, he thought. His old pain-lined face would just tighten and he would say little, only dig in and plan a way to try again.

Moss Dean worked his mount alongside. The broad shadow of him leaned quite near, so Moss did not have to raise his voice. "Your idea of night travel," said Moss, "was good. But not good enough."

Brazos jerked a backward glance to the darkness. He could not see beyond Red Myrick's plodding shadow.

Moss asked, "You feel what I feel?"

"Maybe. Now that you've mentioned it."

"Wouldn't hurt to find out now."

"There's an arroyo just ahead. Cedar growth."

They slowed and Red caught up. Brazos told him, "Moss thinks we're followed."

"No need to tell me. I got ears."

Brazos thought that if the three of them had sensed the same thing it must be so. The turf beneath the horses' hoofs cushioned sounds. The riders back there could draw very near without much noise.

"When we hit the cedars, keep riding a distance. I'll drop to the side and take a stand in the brush. If they come by, I'll get a look. If you hear commotion, you can move in on the other side. Got it?"

"And if it's fifty drunk Comanche bucks," Red grunted, "well, glad to have knowed you gents."

Brazos pulled off beside the trail, dismounted, and shielded himself and the mustang behind a cedar stand. The sounds of Moss's and Red's horses drifted out of his hearing through the straggle of big cedars.

The forms of three horsemen materialized from the west. From these three, one came ahead alone, gradually looming larger, and two held back in the shadows. Opposite Brazos' concealment the single rider pulled up as casually as if they were meeting here by appointment.

"You would be about yonder," a voice called out. "Will you come around here, please?"

Brazos stayed frozen, but there was no use. They had heard the horse sounds change, and this one knew a man had dropped out.

The boyish voice added, almost apologetically, "I'm Jack Hays."

"All right, damn it, Hays. What do you want?"

The youthful figure eased his seat and pulled one leg comfortably cross-saddle. He had not drawn rifle or revolver.

"You McCloud, I take it. Which one?"

"Brazos."

"Wid's brother?"

"The same. You fought together."

"I remember."

"Now, shall we talk about the weather a while, or annexation?"

"You the man we're looking for?"

"You ought to know."

"Ought to, but don't. Got a what-you-call-it, a-nono-mus rumor, with a McCloud name hooked on the end of it."

"Well, get to the point, Captain."

"Who's riding with you?"

He saw no use to lie. These were the Rangers and they would be straight from Austin with a purpose, and the purpose wrote out trouble, bold and black in the mocking starlight. He saw the end of all his efforts and plans fray out, there in the person of the commander of the Texas Rangers —a man no older than himself, but nobody to trifle with for damn-sure certain. Brazos said, "Moss Dean and Red Myrick."

Hays whistled. "You got some right able *compadres.*" He swung his arm high. His two companions came from the darkness where they had covered him. Hays said to them, "The other two will ambush you a ways ahead. Bring them back."

"In what condition, Captain?"

"Just tell 'em I want 'em," Hays said patiently. "One of them is Moss Dean. Better speak up pronto when you flush him."

The two rode ahead. Hays said, "You want to bring your horse around here?"

Brazos got his mount and led it back. Hays had dismounted. He extended a hand to Brazos and they shook. Then Hays ran his fingers across the bulge along the saddle roll. "What's in here?"

"What does it feel like?"

"Money. How much?"

"One thousand dollars in gold."

Hays whistled again. "Now what'd you know! Where'd it come from?"

"I took a few eggs to town."

"Hens must be doin' well. They laid any valuable papers of some kind?"

"No papers. Why?"

Hays tilted his hat and let out a low oath. "This is a

cockleburr assignment if there ever was one. Every job they give the Rangers is a funny one. How's Wid?"

"His stump usually hurts. Otherwise, all right, last time I saw him."

"He was fightin' under Old Paint that time, I remember, when we took on the Mexicans at Salado. Woll fair got away from us and picked up those prisoners in Sanantone. Any word from your pa?"

Brazos shook his head. Were they going to take him back or weren't they? Hays remarked, "They sent us all the way from Austin. The Secretary of State. You got some papers or something?"

"I said no, once."

"Guess not, now. Not with a thousand in gold. Already paid for and delivered. What in hell was it all about? You know what they're saying in Austin about your pa."

"You tell me."

Jack Hays shrugged and got on his horse. "Whether he's a traitor is not for me to decide." Brazos mounted, too. The other Rangers came back in a minute, flanking Moss and Red.

"Hello, Moss. Where you boys headed?"

"We're headed home," Brazos said. "To my place."

Hays was silent for a moment. Then, "You reckon you ought to ride to Austin with me, McCloud? I'm just asking."

"No good reason I can think of."

"They's a big stink. That's a good reason. Sam Houston —that's another good reason. He's curious."

Moss wanted to know: "What led you on to us, Jack?"

"Things we picked up around Sanantone when we got in. What's about a doctor? Mexican spy, maybe?"

"Look, Captain," Brazos said. "I've got gold here. My father may be up with the Comanches. Some of the Perote prisoners were released and they brought word that others have been traded to the tribes. I don't know anything about stolen papers. We're planning to head north with the money and try to make a ransom. You want to tell the Secretary of State something, you tell him that if rumor comes to me, just accidentally, of course, on what might be in the documents, and if it's important to the Republic, he'll be the first to know. Fair enough?"

After a moment's hesitation, Hays replied, "I'd say so. Sounds reasonable. We've had a long ride, didn't know a damn thing when we started and won't when we get back, it's the way the gov'ment works. Can't blame you McCloud people for doin' what you can to buy your pa out of captivity, in spite of that treason talk. No, it's a sorry mess, all around. Don't hardly know what we ought to do.

"Now let's see how we stack up here," he went on thoughtfully. "Moss, you and Myrick ain't wanted, that I know of. We'll take Brazos back to Sanantone, and maybe that'll be the end of it. Goddamit, you know I can't just ride back and say I turned him loose. You two can ride on to the McCloud place, if you want to. But we've had a long pull and I suggest we camp right around here for the rest of the night. We haven't et much or slept in near forty-eight hours."

Brazos led the way to a thin timber stand off the trail where the sluggish trickle of a spring provided campsite water. The Rangers unrolled their packs and brought out cold rations; they had agreed in a few words that a fire would be a bad idea, considering that Cherokee horse thieves were often on the prowl this far south. Hays stayed glumly silent as they ate, and so did Brazos, his thoughts working ahead to what might happen to him once he was returned to San Antonio. He could think of no way they could prove anything. Not unless the Spider and Trakken got themselves involved. But there would be delay, and official rigmarole, and his thousand dollars might be taken from him. And in that time, the wily Driscolls might be stealing out of the country with the Union documents.

When the others went to stake their horses for the night it occurred to Brazos that Hays had not bothered to disarm the three of them. Moss Dean came close to Brazos as they picketed their horses in the darkness and mumbled from the side of his mouth, "Put the saddle back on your mount."

"Why?"

"Jack's suggestion."

"Hays said that?"

"Yeah."

"In case of Indians?"

"Dammit—do I have to knock you down with it? He don't want the other two to know."

He understood, only half believing. "You'll meet me at the ranch?"

"Yeah. But lay low somewhere tomorrow in case Jack goes through the motions of hunting you."

In the thick, dark hour before the false dawn, Brazos

quietly slid from his blankets, made his roll, and walked noiselessly to his mustang. He tied on the roll and his precious bag of money, led the horse a distance, mounted, and rode at a walk up the dark bottom of a sandy creek. He knew as well as if he had seen him that Jack Hays's eyes had followed every move. The officials might rawhide the Ranger back at headquarters for letting his man get away, but he was Jack Hays and nobody would ride him very hard. Brazos holed up in the brush before dawn, figuring his distance from home as no more than three or four hours. He went to troubled sleep, wondering if he would find the Driscolls there at the next nightfall.

VI

If Neches was known for the fantasies of her childish dreams, Brazos was haunted by private visions of his own because he was the McCloud who had seen it happen. Then twenty-three, he was the one who had stood and watched when the Mexican soldiers took his father. More than the others, because of what his eyes had seen happen and his brain remembered, he felt secret torment. Some nights he thought he heard his father's voice and saw again Seale's last look. Seale had turned back to him, where he stood rooted and tear-blinded in the stunned crowd in the plaza. Some nights this last look came back as a far-off expression of impudent bravado, as if Seale meant to grin and nuzzle a kindly fist under Brazos' chin to give him reassurance. Seale's powerful shoulders would then hunch in a gesture of so-long, and don't worry, boy. A dozen farewell messages and instructions, the only way he could wave goodby, in just the shoulder gesture. His hands were chained to the two prisoners stumbling along on either side.

The sight of his father in the brutal control of other men was an unholy thing in Brazos' troubled dreams. Seeing a man like his father degraded with chains. God! He had *seen* it! The last look back by big Seale and the chains clanking. Seale who had worn his freedom as a prairie wore its distance, now a captive of other men, poked by their bayonets, clubbed down when he spoke, clubbed to his feet when he fell.

These were the half-sleep nightmares that returned to devil Brazos in midafternoon in his thicket hideout. A ground squirrel rustled up, then departed, and Brazos, hearing the rustle, came wide awake. The sun still bounced brassy yellow off the upthrusting, mesquite-thick ridges to westward when he rode to the head of a brushy valley. Working his horse down to the mesquites below, he was halfway to the bottom when a movement flashed somewhere in the distant valley. The specks, when he first caught them, were emerging from a brushy hollow at the far end of the sink. One running horse was all he saw at first. In the space of three slow breaths he saw the other three emerge, and he knew that this was a chase.

The three far back were Indians. The one coming ahead was the quarry. Then the fleeing rider came into better vision and Brazos felt an invisible fist smash him in the stomach. *This one was a girl.*

The thought that she might be one of his sisters dried out his mouth. The copper-hued bodies, low-bent to barebacked mustangs, were gaining on her. Brazos yelled into the ear of his mustang and drove in his spurs. He yanked his rifle from its boot and rode hard for the valley brush.

He marked the direction of the girl's course and headed diagonally to intercept it. The Indians, strung out a little, had anticipated it, too, and he saw that they were going to close in. But he would reach her first and the intervening mesquites would shield him for another minute.

When he made the interception, the fleeing rider came out of the brush, bent low in her saddle and wildly kicking her horse. With astonishment, he saw she was not one of his sisters, but the San Antonio girl, the doctor's daughter—Risa Driscoll.

He made a quick signal, urging her to keep the course on which she was headed toward the snubnosed mounds and rocky upthrusts of the Coronado faults. Plenty of concealment up there, if they could make it.

When the lead Indian came into view, Brazos waited until the range closed. His finger squeezed slowly on the rifle trigger. He tried to hold the bead on the dark blur of the running pony. The Indian kept coming for six wild jumps and then the pony swerved abruptly as if meeting a stone wall. The rider did not lose his perch and Brazos had to figure the shot a failure. He loaded and triggered another shot at the next pony, then all three were lost to sight in the brush. He spurred his mustang and soon caught sight of Risa. He mo-

tioned left, to the jagged upthrust of the rocky shelf and
chaparral growth.

They came together where the steep ridge raised to rocky
cliffs. He called, "Keep riding! Up the ridge!"

They reached the higher boulders and dwarf brush where
he took both horses and tied them in cover. Far out the Indian ponies showed, vanished, showed again. Cherokees, all
right. Young bucks, likely, from the tame camp on the Cibolo. Not so tame but what they could be troublesome, though.
He crawled to Risa in the dry grass tufts. She whispered,
"They have gone away, you think?"

"Not yet. They're having too much fun."

"Dios! That is *fun?"*

Now he felt delayed irritation rising. "Three Cherokee
boys and a white girl. To an Indian, that's fun. What fool
thing are you doing out here?"

She had a sharpness in her voice to match his own. "What
am I doing? Running like a bantam *gallina* in a strange barn-
yard—what did it appear to you?"

"I mean, why are you out here alone?"

"Then ask me like a gentleman."

"Good God, we don't have time for an etiquette lesson!
First, what about the pouch, my papers? Did you bring
them?"

The strain of her flight at last overcame her composure.
He saw her twist her lithe body until she lay stretched with
her face in her arms. He looked away as her shoulders began
shaking. The muffled sobs came. He knew female reaction to
a bad thing, and to give her dam burst time to spend itself
he crawled out a distance. He found a gun rest between two
flinty rocks. Soon he found movement in the brush below,
three dabs of copper and feathers. The fun was not yet over
for the young Cherokees, apparently. They were out of rifle
range, headed for the same rise as this rocky ridge. They
would want to gain higher ground, to work their way down
for a try from above.

He crawled back to the cedars. "Come on. Higher in the
boulders." When the brush thickened he tied the horses and
climbed along the cliffside. He found an eroded cutback in
the white sandstone, forming a shallow cave with a ceiling
that would clear a bent-down man. He made a quick look inside for rattlers, then called to Risa.

She scurried under the shale overhang. Brazos returned to

concealment behind the boulders. Sun shadows played confusingly over the roughs. He watched for any cross-movement, some bend in the brush. He fitted the rifle butt to his shoulder. When the next color showed itself he brushed as gently on the trigger as Risa had fingered off her tears, and the blast rattled the cliffside. He loaded and fired again while the echo still rebounded from the rocky heights. The brush bent in a flurry of running figures. He fired one more slug into their retreating scramble.

Now the young Cherokees could regroup somewhere in safety below for whatever manner of juvenile war parley they might be moved to hold—with a verdict, he hoped, that it would be unwise to risk the dangers above during the coming dark hours. He would let the daylight situation take care of itself when it came.

Risa peered from the opening. When he joined her she drew away and rested her back against the opposite wall.

"Those shots?"

"Just something to discourage them. You all right now?"

"They will be worried about me."

"Who will be worried?"

"My father. Your family."

"You have been to our homestead?"

"Since yesterday. I rode from there this afternoon. Teche let me have the horse."

"What for? Where were you going? Didn't you know enough not to come riding this way alone? Didn't they tell you about the Cherokees?"

"Please! I am not up to an argument. Later, when I am over this—I will be glad to argue."

But Brazos could delay the question no longer: "Where is my document pouch? Did you bring it?"

Their eyes dueled across the small space, and suddenly he moved across the sand, close upon her, filled with anger and impatience. "Now, listen. I'm tired pussyfooting with you damned people! By God, I want to know what you did with my property after you stole it, where it is now, and what it takes to get it. Otherwise—"

The force of his words made her press against the wall. But he saw the thin white line of her teeth showing, her challenging smile.

"Otherwise—what?"

Brazos didn't know. He relaxed, baffled; his threat had swollen inside the cave like a sun-puffed gourd and collapsed in the same way. The burst fragments of it lay all around. He drew back to his side of the cave.

"I'd know if you were a man. I'd soon get those papers."

"Are they so important?"

"To me, they are. Why did you steal them?"

"I spied on you," she said flatly. "When you hid the pouch under the mattress I nearly died of curiosity. I knew when you left by the window, so I went in and rooted out the pouch to see what it could possibly be. Was that so wrong? Then the soldiers came. It was lucky I had time to hide it in another place. I have wondered—you meant to come back for it?"

"I did. Where I was going I preferred not to have it with me. Not until I collected."

"Oh! So there is *dinero* in this! *Origen de maldad!* I thought so."

"You know any other root of evil that will take its place in these times? At least, nothing but money will do for the purpose this was intended." Then, wearily, "I thought you did not wish to argue. It will save your breath if you will just say *where* the blasted pouch is." He remembered this was something of the way Trakken had exploded. He could better sympathize now with Trakken's frustration. He could also see, in the light of what had happened, that Trakken and the Spider would never have paid him if he had carried the documents to them that night. For once, at least, he had played a hunch right.

"I think you should know," he said, "that this involves money that may buy back a man's life. This man is in living death, even now, and he has a family that dies a little every sundown, from the strain of wondering."

"I know!" Risa murmured. "I have heard this from your sisters. Yesterday we talked, Sabine and Neches and Ann. They have been kind to me. I like your *familia.*"

"Then you would have liked our father best of all. He is himself, and also he is all of us."

He brought in his gear and tossed the blanket to her and opened the canteen. He took out the wrapped tortillas and the cold frijoles in corn husks that Red Myrick's wife had packed for them, passing food to her. He placed the money-bag at his side against the wall.

After a time, Risa said, "I would like to hear more, about your father, if it does not unduly pain you to speak of it."

He washed down a flabby tortilla and remembered the

morning Seale was taken away. Then, seeing it again, as vivid as his last nightmare, he told her.

That Sunday morning had been a sunny one and Brazos had awakened in their room on the plaza to strange sounds and smells, feeling important to be in so much town bustle. Tomorrow, Seale was to be a juror in a case in court. He had brought Brazos on the long day's journey into town just for the trip, because Brazos had not been to the Bexar settlement for many months. Wid was away riding with Old Paint Caldwell's troops and Teche had stayed on the claim to look after the girls. But the pleasure of the town visit with his father was short-lived. Within five minutes after his awakening, the roar of cannon fire shook the adobe walls of the inn, and the sounds outside his window turned into yells of alarm and many running feet.

"How they slipped into town, nobody ever knew," he told Risa. "All at once there was cannon fire, then Mexican soldiers. Soldiers afoot and soldiers mounted. It turned out that General Woll had fourteen hundred of them and they took full control.

"My father went to where some citizens were gathering. That was when General Woll sent his men to round up everyone in the Council House. These men were in town for the court session. The Mexicans took them all: the judge, attorneys, jurors, and witnesses, just for the whim of doing it. Fifty-nine men were in that one bunch, besides some other prisoners.

"All at once these men were captives, herded down the street by soldiers using bayonets and sabers. I saw one get his head sliced in half because he tried to hold back. You couldn't find anyone to answer a question, and the Mexican officers gave orders for the people to stay inside their houses.

"Woll pulled out with some of his force and his artillery, because they had word that the Texas soldiers were coming up the Salado. That battle was where Wid got his leg shot off. The Mexicans retreated back into San Antonio two days later and they were in a hurry by then. I had not seen my father until the Mexican army began its retreat to the border."

He paused. Risa spoke quietly, "That was when you saw —the chains?"

"You would have to know him."

"But I understand!"

"I wonder. Can you understand that the Spaniards will torture other humans just because they like to see suffering, and no better reason needed? It is their nature. They have had generations of Roman priests saying prayers over them, but they still will go out and enjoy doing what they do to their captives. I've wondered, where do their officers cache the dried ears of the Texans they have mutilated when they go in for confessions?"

"Just the military ones!" she said quickly. "Like Santa Anna's soldiers."

"Most Mexicans."

"No!"

"To inflict pain is something in their blood," Brazos insisted.

She smoothed her dress with studied care and said distantly, "My mother was a Mexican."

"Then I was not speaking of your mother."

"What was yours?"

"She—it doesn't matter. A schoolteacher. One thing she taught us was that hearts were all the same color. I am not speaking of the bastards as nationalists. I'm speaking only of a breed like Woll's army that will torture men from the other side when they get them captured. Who but the Spanish have the taste for that? The Apaches, maybe."

In a moment, Risa said slowly, "But she was married to your father, at least. You do not carry the only curse in the land."

"The only curse?"

"Oh, I do not worry." She laughed shortly. "Did I have anything to do with it?"

"To do with what?"

"My birth."

He peered hard at her across the gathering dusk of the cave. "Who was *your* mother?"

"That doesn't matter, either. Yours was a schoolteacher. Well, mine was the doctor's friend in Vera Cruz. My father loved her, he now says. They just forgot to see a priest."

"Why do you tell me this?"

"Only because—" She folded her hands in her lap. The shadows were heavy now, with the sunlight nearly gone. He could no longer see her eyes. "You have been sad and what you tell me makes me sad. Perhaps it is sympathy that I feel. That you should know others have their little stickers in the bed, same as you, to keep them awake in the long nights.

"But your father," she prompted. "Would you care to tell me more about that?"

He tilted his head back to the sandy wall and spoke through a tired drowsiness. "He had the yonder horizons in his eyes, and travel in his feet. Which is why we moved so often. When the woodpile ax had grown dull by spring-time he would rather move again to a new land claim than sharpen the bit for chopping once more where the stand was already cut over. He wanted virgin trees to sink the ax into, over the next range of hills, on another river, and to puddle new 'dobe bricks from virgin mud."

"In Mexico there was no mud like that," she murmured. "Nor women. Where there are always soldiers, there is not much virgin anything."

"There is such a thing as new mud." He wanted her to understand. "Clean earth for the house bricks. Seale said, who wants to live within walls that feet have walked all over and somebody's hogs once wallowed in? That's why he always looked to the next land grant west of where we might be, and it kept the western distance in his looks and talk. And nobody knew what was in his heart, unless it was a song that disguised the pain after my mother died. So he looked for new hills, and new clay for cabin adobe, and when she lived, for a baby and a new river to name it for. That was the man the Mexican soldiers made walk in leg irons all the way from San Antonio to a Perote dungeon. While the Mexicans rode and shot in the back those who crippled and stumbled along the way."

"Brazos—I wish you had told me, when you were at our house—that you had not slipped away," she said after a moment.

"Nobody I would trust in that town!" he retorted. "Somebody spread the report that my father gave out Army secrets to the Mexicans in return for favors. The lie has been spread, and now even the state officials will do nothing to help buy him back from the Comanches. Do you think if he gave help to the Mexicans they would have traded him to the Indian tribes up here?"

"But you have to trust *somebody*," she protested.

"Not in the kind of thing I got mixed up in when I went to San Antonio. I had to raise money, somehow. Wid told me when I left home—he warned me. He said, 'The only women I trust are under this roof, Teche's wife, Sabine, and Neches —you get away from your own house and women are apt to have your brain limpin' on a hurtin' stump like this bob-tailed leg of mine. They've got the soft riggin' for taking you in.' That was Wid's last advice to me."

"It is not so! Wid is hurt inside, because of his leg. Ann told me—he has no business trying to make the trip north with you and Teche. He will be more of a burden than help. But all of you said he might go, because you know he will rot inside himself if he is made to stay. But you must not believe Wid on—on this other thing. When his leg went, all women from then on went out of his life, because he was—well, too proud. What he said to you, that is not fair!"

"Turned out *verdico!*" he said dryly. "Who but a woman stole my property and made bad trouble for me?"

"The soft riggin' part, I mean!" she retorted with emphasis. "As Wid calls it. I didn't use *that!*" She made a small gasp, then, and he supposed if he could see her well enough he would see a blush. "Anyhow," she said primly, "if I hadn't moved the document pouch the soldiers would have found it. So I was of little help."

It was time to crawl outside and look over the night. He did this, listening for a long time. The horses munched with a faintly-heard scissoring of the tough grass. He would have ridden for home, now, under other circumstances. But not with Risa here and the Cherokees somewhere down the slope. When he came back inside the cave he saw her dark form stretched upon the blanket. He settled against the wall again with the rifle across his legs and watched the purple evening beyond the opening.

She turned on her side with her head cradled upon her arm. Her free hand smoothed the ridges of the unoccupied half of the coarse blanket. "Is your wound hurting now?"

He said, "No." A horned frog appeared from beneath the disturbed sand and fled for the light shaft at the opening, its flat head raised and its spread legs churning in retreat as if it were shamed by its own ugliness. He saw a crusty hide of warts slither down the wall cracks and come out in the gravel, to be joined by its lizard mate, and the two scuttled like a yoked team for some other eroded crevice. He took a swallow of the canteen water. He slid his long frame upon the nearer edge of the blanket and stretched tiredly, facing her only three feet away, and adjusted his arm under his dull-throbbing shoulder.

"A few of the Santa Fe expedition prisoners have been released. Wid went to talk to them. They told how it was, and they denied that my father had committed treason while in Mexico, but the stain is still on his name at Austin. These prisoners told how they were captured by Governor Armijo in New Mexico, another beast like Woll. The first thing the Mexicans did up there was to march two of the Texas leaders out to the plaza in San Miguel. They tied their hands behind them and made them kneel and shot them in the back with all the people watching. That was just for a lesson to the other Texas prisoners. They walked these most of the time, all the way down to the City of Mexico, over a thousand miles. If a man grew sick or lame, they shot him. So we know how it was with the Santa Fe prisoners and wonder how it might have been with the San Antonio men that Woll captured. Have you heard what they did with the Mier captives? The black beans?"

He sensed the small shudder that went over her. "Yes! I do not wish to hear that told again! Everyone in Texas has had their sleepless hours, thinking of such brutality."

"All right, Risa." He felt his throat thicken. "My father was a man who loved free movement so much that he tried to wade in it up to his chin, like creek water to splash in. Now he is a captive of the tribes, we think. The documents were for the money that was to pay the ransom for his release, if we can contact the right Comanche bunch. I am honor bound to deliver the pouch to my confederates. It means a thousand dollars to me."

He reached his foot to touch the Spider's canvas money bag, and felt the gold coins give to the pressure. The time was come to pay her the price, if she was ready to name it. He thought he knew what all the curious *locuacidad* of the girl's had been leading to. In all that talk she had sought to discover how important the documents were to him and what he might be forced to pay.

"You said you and the doctor must have money to travel on, now that they've run you out of the settlement. So I ask you—what is your price?"

She rose quickly on her elbow. The movement caused a swish of cloth sounds and a stirring down the length of her body. His vision adjusted to the darkness, her profile took outline, her bare throat, and the shape of her rumpled bodice. Her face was very near.

"I have no price, Brazos."

"You mean you don't have the papers?"

"Oh, I have them! I hid them on the journey to your homestead. I left the wagon once and hid the pouch under some stones. This was where the old tracks turned from the Cibolo, and the place I hid it was beneath three fat oak trees standing by themselves near the crossing. Do you know the place?"

"I know it."

"I did not tell my father when I came back to the wagon. I was not sure what it was I wished to do. I thought to ask some pay, yes. I had something valuable, I knew, and we were in bad need of money. But now I have known your sisters, and Wid and Teche. And you— So they are yours, and there is no price."

She lapsed into silence. He reached out his hand to touch her profile, to brush the hair strands back from her cheek. She did not move. The cave seemed to close in on him like a smothering of bedclothes and the blanket beneath them seemed to shrink to pigmy size. He had the feeling that there was danger of falling from its woven edges to yawning dark depth dropping below to infinity. Her breath touched his skin, and she spoke again. "Now I know the McClouds and what you propose to do with the money, this plan about traveling north to find your father. You can have the documents. We will drive on, *my* father and I, to some new place."

Brazos touched her cheek again. Then, compelled to, he extended his good arm until it lay across her shoulder. His small pressure brought a stop in her breathing and a restraining rigidness that he felt. He knew her look sought his face questioningly. He tried to draw her tightly to him, oblivious to his wound bandage grinding into the sand under the blanket.

"I—I think I heard the sound of someone outside," Risa whispered.

He had heard no sound. But he withdrew his arm, got up, and crawled out with the rifle. He watched and listened for a while, and there was no sound at all except those safely belonging to the night.

When he returned, she was fast asleep, or pretended to be, rolled completely in the blanket. He stretched in the sand and listened to a distant coyote pair taking on under the quarter moon.

VII

In September, the Texas sun projected an hour of woolly daylight over the purplish, sleeping land before it cracked the eastern ridges with its fire. It was this first gray light that nudged Brazos out of the gentlest oblivion he had ever known. Risa, in her blanket cocoon, was backed against him, both their bodies pulled into one pressing knot from the chill. Moving his legs, cramped with cold, he took some care lest he awaken her.

The horses were all right, though fretting for feed and water; the Cherokee boys, so far as any signs showed, had decided to head for home. As he saddled he saw Risa emerge, looking like an Indian girl coming from a tepee. She carried the blanket roll and his moneybag. Her brown features sought him in an impassive look, then a small white show of teeth broke the set of her lips. He met her as she came down to the horses and took the load from her arms. Her dress could never be ironed smooth again, he thought, nor her hair straightened of its tangles. They mounted and suddenly seemed far apart, as visions of home and family filled his mind.

He said briefly, "I'm glad you don't want pay for the documents. But I thought you and your father might wish to remain at our place while we're gone to Torrey's Post. If you desire to."

"Thank you. We'll see. I don't know what my father will want to do."

They began the descent into the gray mist of dewy mesquites. Far off to the northeast, as the last thing visible before the brush blocked his view, he sighted the scrawly line that was the tree growth along the Cibolo. Over there at the gravel crossing would be the triple oaks that marked the hiding place of his stolen Union pouch. And straight-up sun would find them home again.

When they came into sight of the homestead, with the recovered document pouch secured to Brazos' saddle, he uneasily felt that a little rehearsal was needed.

"It would be just as well," he told Risa, "if we said that you hid from the Indians last night and that I ran across you this morning where you were recovering the pouch on the creek."

She retorted, "There was nothing wrong!"

"It would be simpler, though."

"Just as you wish."

Neches sighted them from the yard and came running, with Sabine quickly following. Then the others trailed out, and the welcome was on.

When the scene in the yard began to blow itself out after a hurricane of questions, Brazos saw Moss Dean and Red Myrick approaching from the barn. Moss greeted the situation with a dark scowl, but Red Myrick turned on a head-bobbling grin for everyone. Teche showed stiff pleasure that Brazos was home. Wid, though his creviced face looked to be stacking questions like cordwood, stood by like a bull buffalo satisfied that the whole herd was now compact on safe graze. Dr. Driscoll came from the house. He put a hand out for an awkward pat to Risa's shoulder, then all the way around for a clumsy hug. The whisky smell on him drifted across to Brazos' notice. The McClouds, as if belatedly remembering, turned to Risa and spoke their pleasure for her safe return and their curiosity as to where she had been.

The scene was getting a little too cozy for Brazos, and he said he had to take care of the horses. As he moved away to take the reins he heard Risa's bland reply to the girls, that she had gone to retrieve something lost on the way. She had sighted Indians and thought it prudent to hide in a cave during the night. He heard Sabine's awed question: "Well, did you find what you went after?" And Risa's smile-touched reply, *"Si, lo hallé, amigas mías, en la caverna."*

Well, maybe he had found himself, too. In the cave. He wanted to look back at her but the men were straggling along in a drift behind him. Teche gave him a hand at unsaddling, watering, and feeding the horses. At last Brazos hoisted the money sack and the government pouch and came face to face with Wid's dark-furrowed scrutiny. Wid and Teche followed him into the shed, away from the others.

Brazos had never lied to Wid in his life. He saw no reason to lie now about the source of the money. He indicated the bag. "It's a thousand dollars. I stole the damn stuff. This is a Union document pouch—I took it off a government messenger in Louisiana. I still have to deliver it to the men who hired me to get it."

Wid put a slow fire to his pipe on that. Teche just stared at him with open curiosity. First, Wid wanted to know about the Rangers. "Jack Hays let you off, according to Moss and

Red. What's from here? They going to be after you or not?"

One did not evade Wid with very much ease. Brazos said, "What he did speaks for itself, doesn't it? But I don't know what Austin will do, how bad they want me. Or these documents. For the last month I've been willing to concern myself with one thing at a time."

Teche remarked that by the time the Texas government could do anything one way or the other, they would already be well on their way north to Torrey's Post, and Wid grunted his agreement. They would make a quick start, now that they had money to work with. But what about his confederates in the deal?

"They're secret agents for somebody—they claim it's England. Could be Mexico. They tried to pull a fake robbery on me, but their man jumped the traces before they had the documents in hand."

They talked this around for a while, and then discussed the details involved in getting ready for the journey north. Wid said that they had arranged for the two Fitzpatrick boys, from the neighboring claim, to stay on the place with the women and look after the cattle while the men were gone.

"You still intend to go, I take it?" Brazos asked.

Wid glared at him. "Why, hell yes! Any reason I shouldn't?"

"Not a reason in the world, Wid."

"Then that'll be the last damn-fool mention of it."

Teche expressed satisfaction that their uncle Moss Dean and Wid's old side-kick, Red Myrick, also would be in the party. "The five of us ought to be able to handle whatever we run into up there. I figure that once we find Bartolo, and let it be known we've got money, that we'll make a contact on those prisoners pretty quick."

The big question hung over them all for a long moment. Would they find Seale McCloud up there?

Wid fingered a bead of sweat off his forehead. "The girl," he mentioned, drying his hand on his pants leg. "She had a fool idea, going off by herself to retrieve that pouch. We told her those half-tame Cherokees were apt to range down this far."

"Smart of her to hide in a cave last night," Teche remarked.

"I reckon you were hid out from the Rangers in the same vicinity and didn't know it," Wid remarked. Brazos shot him a hard look. "Rangers after you, Cherokees after her." Wid maneuvered himself erect. "You and Risa must have been hiding closer to one another than you thought. Noticed both of you had slept with your heads in that white mealy sand like up there on Catclaw Ridge."

Guiltily, Brazos started to reach his hand to his hair, then stayed it. The Catclaw Ridge sand was whiter than any other sand in the country. He felt Wid's shrewd scrutiny and picked up the pouch, changing the subject. "Soon as Driscoll dresses my shoulder, we need to open this and go through the documents."

Wid said soberly, "It would make a hell of a problem if these papers are something that'd be useful to Sam Houston. It would be up to us to deliver them to Austin."

Teche objected, "You seem to be making it that we decide which comes first, the Texas cause or Pa. Well, it wouldn't take me long to decide *that*."

"Thing is, Brazos owes these papers to his partners. Else the money goes back."

"Well, he stole the papers, didn't he? What's the difference?"

"That was from the Union, Teche," said Brazos. "The money is different. It's pay for a job and I've given my word they'll get the documents. There's more than that. Captain Spide has information from Torrey's Post, he claims. May be the means for us to make a contact up there."

"The bastards tried to rob you."

Wid said, "Makes a hell of a hard thing to decide. If these are documents that Sam Houston could profit by seeing, the papers have got to go to Austin and the money back to Brazos' partners."

Teche gritted, "And we forget about Pa? You mean that?"

Brazos knew where he was going. He stared them both down. "I'm making the trip north and I'm taking the money with me. I'm too far gone in this to worry about anything else."

Wid said, "Well, maybe it's no problem. Let's look at the documents, then we'll know." But by now, the nibble of dread had been started in Brazos. Suppose, as Wid said, the documents contained information of vital importance to the Texas government?

When Brazos brought the government pouch into the kitchen and placed it upon the table, the action drew all the others like the sounding of a dinner bell. By the time Brazos worked his knife blade into the wax seals, the kitchen was crowded.

Sabine exclaimed, "It's something like Christmas morning, isn't it?"

The packages came out, small wrapped bundles of assorted papers. Wid said, "You do the honors. Start reading."

Handling papers that had had their ink put to them in far-off Washington, maybe in the White House itself, for all he knew, did something to Brazos' blood like the first jolting shot of mescal. He remembered again how the government messenger had taken on during the robbery. Teche's impatience, at that point, could not be contained; he moved to help himself to a serving of the papers in front of Brazos. Wid quickly said, "No, let's have just one working on it, so all of us will be knowing the same thing at the same time and not getting mixed up." Teche, flustered, tossed the papers back. Brazos scanned the pages to get his bearings and began to give the others the gist of what he read as quickly as he could digest it.

"Most of these seem to be written to a man named William Murphy, the chargé d'affaires for the Union at Austin. This one says the United States has discovered that Sam Houston is negotiating with England to use force against Mexico and to lend money to the Republic, which we all knew. Main thing here, though, it says Texas is trying to influence some of the Southern slave states to throw in with us and make a new nation that will even overshadow the Union. Which *would* be something, wouldn't it?"

He glanced up to see beaming faces everywhere, except from the Driscolls. Wid muttered, "That's a grandiose plan, one I hadn't heard about to now. Old Sam is a foxy one."

Brazos continued: "Now in this note, they're telling Murphy where they got some of this information, which is from the office of the Secretary of State himself. They managed to obtain—they don't plain say 'stole'—some communications from Houston to our commissioners in Washington, Henderson and Van Zandt."

Sabine made a face. "*Stole* our messages! How do you like that?"

Wid drawled, "Plain coyote, anyone who would steal documents." Moss and Red chuckled.

Brazos went on, giving them the information as soon as he could put it together from his rapid reading of the papers.

The British agent in Texas, Captain Charles Elliott, was directed to work out a peace treaty between Mexico and

Texas, so the hard-pressed Republic would be freed of constant war threat. "There's a great tension between Washington and England over that issue," Brazos said. "Listen to this—they're also having a dispute about boundaries in the Northwest and on seizure of slave ships off the African coast. Fact is, there's a strong possibility of war between the Union and England this minute."

Wid whistled. "Wouldn't Houston be interested in knowing *that!*"

"Here's one from Secretary Upshur, relaying a message to Murphy direct from President Tyler. Tyler instructs Murphy to tell Houston, 'Please encourage your people to be quiet and not grow impatient for annexation, we are doing all we can to annex you to the United States but we must have time.' "

"Like a three-legged race at a fandango," Moss remarked. "The Union, England, and Mexico. The one that doesn't fall and bust himself thinks he's won us."

Brazos said, "This one is headed 'Very Confidential.' It says that they think some leaders in Britain want to offer us the money to reimburse all the Texas slaveholders if we will abolish slavery in the Republic, and then they would make war on Mexico to force Santa Anna to recognize us as an independent country."

Ann complained, "It's getting so mixed up that I wouldn't be able to say what we *should* do about it!"

"If it mixes us up," said Teche, "think how they're mixed up in Washington."

"Here's something that shows to be a copy of what their Secretary of State, this Abel P. Upshur, wrote to President Tyler himself—they wanted their Texas agent to know about it. Upshur has said to Tyler, 'Few calamities could befall this country more to be deplored than the establishment of a predominant British influence and the abolition of domestic slavery in Texas. Texas would soon outrank the Union not only in size but as a world power.' "

As that weighty potentiality sank in, the group fell completely silent. This was broken at last by Wid, a hoarsely triumphant throb of satisfaction in his tone: "That settles it! We've got them on the run! Texas will never fall for any more of that annexation talk, and we'll stay a free Republic, maybe twice as big as the Union before it's over! All we have to do is hold out a little longer against those Northern politicians!"

Brazos said, "President Houston seems to agree with you. Listen to what he has written Secretary Upshur—they're sending their Austin envoy a copy. The old chief told 'em, 'Whatever the desires of the Texas government or the people are, or might have been, in relation to annexation, I am satisfied that they're not ambitious at this time, nor will ever be again, to be seen in an attitude of a bone of contention, to be worried or annoyed by the influence of conflicting politicians.' "

Moss said soberly, "Houston is no fool. He sees the vision we see. Texas the greatest nation on the earth, with the Pacific lapping our Western shore. If only the fools in this country can come to see it, too, and drop this annexation foolery. Bunch o' weaklings, some of them."

The others joined with a rush into these rosy speculations, but Brazos was reading something that caused him to lift a hand for silence. "Listen to this!" He felt his eyes burn. "The Union has got hold of a message Houston wrote to Santa Anna on that threat to invade us, and evidently it's one more thing to put the good Secretary of State up in the air. Here's how Houston invited Mexico to do her worst—and I gather the Union is afraid war will break out all over and that England will take a hand.

" 'Eight years ago you were a suppliant; obtained your liberation without ransom, and acknowledged the government of Texas,' Houston is saying to Santa Anna. Then he says—"

"That was when he had him a prisoner over yonder in the marshes," Wid nodded. "Remember him that day, Moss?"

"Whipped cur, if ever was one!"

Brazos read on from the Houston letter to the Mexican president: " 'If Texas existed then as a nation, her recognition since by other powers, and increased commercial relations, will excuse your recognition now of her sovereignty. But, Sir, you speak of your resources and power. They were defied and triumphed over in 1836, and if you invade Texas in 1844, you will find neither her powers nor the success of her arms less complete.' "

Teche remarked, "I hear England's voice somewhere back of all that bravery."

Brazos said, "But he's only beginning to put the spurs to the great general down in Mexico. Houston goes on, 'I desire to know for what reason you have charged the authorities of Texas with perfidy. Have they given to Mexico any pledge they have not redeemed? They have liberated her chiefs and soldiers taken on the field of battle, without obligations to do so. . . .' "

Moss Dean muttered, "A mistake it was, too."

" 'But they are a race which permit neither their word nor their honor to be falsified. How has it been with Mexico? The capitulation of Fannin was disregarded, and hundreds massacred in cold blood. . . . Of the inoffensive traders who visited Santa Fe, and capitulated to your officers, what was the treatment? They were slaughtered by the wayside, when unable to march, and their ears cut off, evidence, indeed, of barbarity not heard of among nations pretending to be civilized since the ninth century of the Christian era.' "

Teche said flatly, "Bestial *bastardos*, all!" Ann murmured a scolding. Brazos shot a glance to Teche and saw him staring directly at Dr. Driscoll. He cut his eyes to see Driscoll's shrug, then Risa's expressionless face, though her lips had drawn a little tight.

Brazos said, "Let's just hear Houston on the subject, Teche."

Teche grinned unpleasantly, started loading his pipe, and looked at nobody.

Sabine whispered, "Are you coming to anything about the San Antonio prisoners, Brazos?" Ann put her arm affectionately about the girl's shoulder.

He shook his head, and resumed reading: " 'Again, at the surrender of Mier, your officers pledged to the men the protection due to prisoners of war, in fulfillment of which, they were soon after barbarously decimated and the remainder ever since held in chains and prison. They were also to be returned to their homes immediately after their submission; but every pledge given them has been violated. Is this good faith?' "

Neches put her head down into her arms on the table and her shoulders convulsed with the sob she tried to stifle. Teche, the nearest, patted her shoulder. Brazos wiped at the sweat that came to his forehead, skipped to the end, and read, " 'You have denounced war, and intend to prosecute it. Do it presently. We will abide the result. Present yourself with a force that indicates a desire of conquest, and with all the appendages of your power, I may respect your effort. But the marauding incursions which have heretofore characterized your molestation will only deserve the contempt of honorable minds.' "

He put the papers aside and glanced around at the tensed

expressions. Red Myrick remarked, frowning, "That last part, I didn't exactly follow."

Wid said, "That's the politician coming out at the last. Flowery way of saying bring on your army, if you've got the guts. What else, Brazos?"

Before he could answer, Driscoll blurted, "Since we're soon to have the Pacific lapping our Western boundary, seems it might call for a little drink of celebration all around!"

"Father!" Risa's cheeks showed red spots.

Moss saved the situation by giving out with, "Amen, Doc!"

Wid kept playing his thick fingers on the table. He looked grim. "The pattern of this whole thing shows one main point. Texas ought to be told that if we can hold out a little longer, we'll have plenty of help from England and we can stay an independent republic. The government at Austin needs to know what we know. Our duty shows clear to me."

"You mean these papers should go to the President?" asked Brazos.

"That's what I mean."

"I've told you I'm honor bound to get these to that pair in San Antonio. It's either that or return the ransom money."

"Why? They tried to double-cross you," Moss reminded.

"Doesn't lessen my obligation. Beside that, we need some information that Captain Spide can give us about Bartolo."

Impatience to start for the north gnawed within Brazos, as it did, he knew, in his brothers. Yet his obligation was plain to deliver what he had been paid for, the merchandise that had put the awesome amount of wealth into their possession and made the ransom attempt miraculously possible. A trade was a trade. The papers must go to Captain Spide and Trakken, even though it was now apparent the tricky pair had meant to rob him of the money almost in the same moment it was paid to him.

He voiced the hazy beginning of an idea. "If there were two sets of these documents, we could do both. One to the Spider, one to Austin."

Dr. Driscoll stalked about, rubbing his chin. "Very simple. Look how many copies of *homo sapiens* have been made out of Eve's one official rib. All you need to do is graft a fresh set of withers to the originals and ride in two directions at once."

"Make a copy!" Brazos nodded. "Why not?"

While they discussed that, Moss took it upon himself to fetch the whisky jug. Driscoll's expression brightened. Moss said he allowed Driscoll could be paid a fee, in this manner if no other, and he would join the doctor in the collection, his throat being parched.

"You're a gentleman, sir," Driscoll said. "A diagnosis I can't apply to all Texans." Red Myrick said that he would like a small fee on account. The upshot was that Ann, who detested to see men drink from the mouth of the gallon earthen jug, brought granite-peeled cups and passed them around. Wid, Teche, and Brazos had their drinks. Brazos tossed the burning jolt to his insides. His shoulder felt fine, after Driscoll's dressing. The doctor had pronounced it almost healed.

"Problem is," Wid said, "how we get the two sets of papers delivered to both San Antonio and Austin. It was my idea for us to get started right off for Torrey's Post."

Brazos remarked that it would be dangerous for himself to be seen in San Antonio. Round-trip travel to Austin would delay them for a week. Nevertheless, the plan required that someone had to go to San Antonio and make contact with Captain Spide and Trakken, and someone had to take a copy of the documents to the capitol.

Risa spoke quietly: "My father can make both journeys for you. Then you will not be delayed on your start."

Driscoll growled, "Me?"

"Yes, father. You can take the papers to the men in Bexar, and then the other set to the capitol."

"Me help this stupid Republic?"

"No. You can help the *McClouds!*" she retorted. "Their father is a captive up there. It is for him."

Driscoll paced like a trapped wolf, his frown deepening, but finally he shrugged in surrender. "I admit a desire to help you people in some way. Though why I would show my face again to that imbecilic militia I don't know. But go ahead. I'll have the papers delivered in both places long before you raise Torrey's Post."

Brazos, feeling quick distrust, said, "You don't have to do this."

"But he *wants* to," said Risa. "Don't you, *padre?*"

"Sure! Sure!" Driscoll jammed his hands into his hip pockets and seesawed. "I've got nothing better to do and nowhere better to go. I hate to admit the softness, but I feel a foolish urge to assist the birth of this peculiar conceivement.

I'll make the deliveries. Then I'd be willing to stay and help the women look after your place. You'll be gone a long time, even with luck. Risa and I are not above doing a little something in exchange for your hospitality."

The others waited for Wid to speak. Privately, Brazos knew, they were all thinking the same question; was Driscoll reliable and loyal to the Texas cause? If the doctor was sympathetic to Mexico he was nobody to trust on the errand. Yet here appeared to be the means of getting the papers sent to where they had to go, with the least delay in the start of their journey.

"We'll make the copies, anyway," said Wid at last. "We'll be considering your offer overnight, doctor." He added gruffly, "Thanks for saying you're willing to help us out."

Driscoll looked as if he could read the doubts in their mind. He tried to square his stooped shoulders and tilted his head with a challenging belligerence. "When I say I'll do a thing, I'll do it!"

Risa knew their doubts, too. She said quietly: "I'll go with him when he takes the documents. I will see that they are delivered—that much we can do, to help a man be freed of his chains."

Wid gazed hard at her. "You will do that? Make the trip to San Antonio, and then to Austin?"

"It's too much to ask," said Brazos quickly. "Besides, the militia in San Antonio—"

"I think I can find your Captain Spide and at the same time dodge the militia," said Driscoll roughly. "Godamighty, folks, it's an offer to help. Otherwise, it doesn't make a bit of difference to me what you do."

Later that night, Wid told Brazos and Teche: "I trust the girl. I think she would see that he did it."

Teche asked, "Would that satisfy you, Brazos? At least you would have *started* the papers to where you say they have to go—looks to me like you could head north then with a clear conscience, or whatever it is that nags you so hard about the damned trade with the Spider."

Brazos thought bleakly that Teche could be an unruly one, at times, and if he was frequently hard to get along with at home, what would he be on the trail when the dangers and hardships turned painful and bad? He said without enthusiasm, "Well, let's get at the job of copying the documents. Let's start Driscoll on his way, and get ourselves started while we've got what harmony there is left to start on."

That night, working at the cleared table, Brazos, Ann and Teche, because their handwritings were judged the best, tediously did the job of copying the documents. The process consumed all the blank paper that could be found in the house, in a variety of scraps and colors. But the words got written and when they had finished there were two sets of the Union documents.

Brazos started for the barn where the men had been bedded in the gear room. Risa appeared on the porch as he stepped into the night. Brazos closed off the kitchen light with a pull on the door.

"I just want you to know," Risa murmured, "that we will do what we say we will—that you need not have that worry, at least, with all the others—when you go north to find him—"

He had the impulsive desire to reach for her, to grasp her and say that he trusted her. He started to do this, knowing with blood-tingling certainty that she would respond to him, that she moved to reach for him, too; then the door opened and he quickly dropped his hands. Teche came out. Brazos moved off, saying roughly, "Yes, the documents are all ready —you and the doctor can head for San Antonio soon as you feel like it."

He started down the dark path to the barn without looking back. Teche, walking behind him, began to whistle a thin, off-key tune through his teeth.

VIII

They drove through a long day, father and daughter, rattling their way back to San Antonio in the same wagon that had carried them out in a degrading retreat, but lighter now since their household belongings had been unloaded at the McClouds'. And their travel mission was gratifyingly different this time, practically an affair of state, Dr. Driscoll commented several times. His long stained fingers handled the lines and the whip with eagerness, urging the team to scramble along.

Government papers to be delivered. Whole turn of the wheel for the Republic might be decided by the Union letters. Queer thing how a man's situation could change over-night, like a fevered child after the crisis, and he told Risa it was a pleasure, a damned funny thing to be doing, after being run out of the settlement, to go back and pull this thing right under the nose of the idiotic Texas militia. That pleases him more, thought Risa, than doing something for the Texas Republic. Their chance acquaintance with Brazos McCloud, coming along with an arrow wound in his shoulder—her father went on—had turned into a quite a thing, hadn't it? Here they were, headed right back to the town that had kicked his name and his practice all over the place with the fool spy talk. Damn it, he *was* anti-United States in the saloons, he guessed, when he'd had a few. He'd never minded telling the windy thick-headed ones that he'd as soon see Texas join up with Mexico again if they had to join somebody. Mexico would be better than the bullying English or the conniving Yankees. Didn't mean he was a spy, though. The other doctor, Jenkins, probably started it all. Jenkins had been to a medical college somewhere and he was a proud and jealous jackass, like most medical doctors with schooling. Sooner or later Jenkins would find out about him, if not already, as had happened other places, and the community would whisper he'd never been trained to doctor anything but dumb animals, and that mostly self-training on Mexico's cavalry stock. Well, let the botfly have 'em. Time out for helping the McCloud bunch suited him just fine. If Risa was willing. The whole thing was a god-send, in a way.

"The girls took a cotton to you, daughter. The men, too. It's me they doubt. A boozer, maybe a spy—I could all but read their minds. Same old story. Your mother was a Mexican, never was a finer woman, never was a better bunch of people than those in Vera Cruz. *Dios!* I thought that we were leaving poverty behind when we shook out of there but we never saw real hard-up broke people till we hit Texas. Risa, I didn't feel the need of you making this trip, though. Oh, I'm glad to have your company, daughter, it's not that, but you made it look to the McClouds— Well, that I needed *watching* over. That you were in the habit of trailing along to see that I did what I was supposed to." He chuckled derisively. "Like I might have got drunk and lost the papers, some fool thing like that." When Risa stayed silent, sitting stiffly at her end of the bouncing wagon seat, he patted her knee forgivingly. "Oh, well, no harm's done, daughter. I am

to Austin while he was away. And she would be waiting when he came back with Seale.

He nuzzled his head to his saddle. The moon broke out where he thought it belonged, a coyote wailed undisturbed, and the breeze arrived untainted by redskin smell, so he guessed the night was organized and ahold of itself. All a man could ask. He slept.

The next night they started shifts of sentry lookouts, drawing lots for each two-hour watch. Wid had an old campaigner's short but pointed say about that. "Don't expect anybody to be that crazy, but one could go to sleep out there five minutes and cost the whole outfit our scalps. It's happened before, could again."

Red Myrick gave out with a mild objection to the direction of their route, repeating some of the things Teche had said. "You're tackin' east of north, Wid—come a blow tonight and we're liable to run aground in Galveston harbor."

Wid chuckled without rancor. "Sea water might taste pretty good, dry as we've been finding the creeks."

Moss said, "When I was up this way that time with the cavalry, we followed the Concho right up to Torrey's with no trouble atall. Of course, Red, they might have moved Torrey's since then, or the Concho River. But if they're where they used to be, we're goin' about right."

"But that was the Texas cavalry," Red grinned. "This here party's *sober*."

Moss laughed with the others. Then Wid told again of the time he and Seale had come as far northwest as two days past the Guadalupe, nearly to the Concho, with a party of prospectors. "I admit we're a shade east, Red, but I was holding to strike water easier this way. Well, if all are agreeable, tomorrow we'll angle west. Soon as we sight the Concho Valley we'll know it and damn well know where we are."

That was the night that Moss Dean came in from the last watch, dew-wet and thoughtful. He propped his rifle to a rock beside the coals, helped himself to a breakfast of venison chunk and fried corn bread, and blew a thoughtful blast at his tin cup of tea. Wid, who was packing his roll nearby, seemed not to look at Moss in the gray dawn, but said quietly, "Speak up, Uncle. What's bothering you?"

"I dunno." Moss chewed steadily for a moment on stringy meat. "Heard something, somewhere. Ponies, maybe. Might have been antelope, though. Maybe just the wind."

That was all Moss had to say. But they rode closed up that day, with saddlebags packed against rattle, and each man with his rifle out of the boot. With the Guadalupe three days behind them, they made a torturous crossing of the canyon land beyond and came to the arid, mesquite-clogged desolation of the dry creeks that fingered out from the Concho Valley. This day they toiled through mesquites, catclaw and brushy dunes without striking a single water hole. They went into a night camp in a cedar-dark arroyo with canteens near empty and the horses hard to manage.

"We'll hit some Concho creek with water in it soon," Wid told them. "Bound to, before much farther."

Teche retorted, "What makes you so damn sure?"

"Why, it just stands to reason. Even if it's been a dry year, they say some of these Concho cuts always hold a little water. Just a matter of finding it."

"Who knows where in hell we are?" Teche argued. "You think we could route ourselves by the sun and still not miss a water hole by a good thirty miles?" He laughed derisively. "You know what I think? I think by God we've been lost since the first day past the Guadalupe."

"I been lost since we left Bexar, myself," said Red Myrick, trying to josh. "Damn me, wouldn't Mealey's beer keg look good now?"

Brazos subdued his own anger at Teche and went off alone with his rifle to pick a cover for the night watch. He moved through the cedars and chaparral, deliberating whether to wet his parched throat or save the couple of swallows of water remaining in his canteen. Soon he was out of hearing of the camp talk.

He saw something move in the dark cedar shadows and stiffened. He strained to watch for the movement, and caught the sounds of dry twigs rustling. Silently, he advanced with the rifle raised. The shadowy figure of a stooped man emerged into an open space leading a saddled mule. Brazos called, "Stand where you are!" The figure stopped. Brazos listened for other sounds, heard none, and advanced. The faint light revealed an old, heavily whiskered face.

Brazos said, "Who are you?"

"Mankin. Name's Mankin. Saw your camp."

"Traveling through, or do you live somewhere about?"

The shaggy figure made an arm motion. "Yonder, apiece."

"How far to water?"

The arm moved again. "Northwest. Up the sink. Half a day."

Brazos was near enough to smell the taint of smoke and old meat, an odor that could only mean Indian. Squaw man. Hide hunter, he guessed.

Moss Dean loomed up. "What've you hooked?"

"Squaw man, from the smell. He might know the rumors of the country, red or white."

"Offer him food."

Mankin volunteered: "Trade a little, up the Concho. You got something to trade for hides? I ain't et lately, either."

"Drift down to camp," said Brazos. "We'll feed you."

Mankin squatted and watched the flames take hold, a cringing creature of hermit silence. Wid and Teche had their try at plying him with questions, but Mankin only withdrew farther into his wariness. Finally Teche snapped with disgust, "You're wasting bread and venison on him, Brazos. Send him on his way."

"Wait a minute," Brazos protested. "Don't rush it so fast." He adjusted the skillet on the coals. "You'll eat, Mankin, when you've answered a few questions. You know Torrey's Post?"

Mankin growled, "Done a little tradin' there."

"What about prisoners? You hear any rumors about white prisoners in the tribes?"

Mankin watched the food browning in the skillet. "Hear a little," he said hoarsely. "White man knows."

"White man? Who is he? Where would we find him?"

Mankin seemed to turn stone deaf. Teche grumbled, "He's making it up," and stalked to his blanket roll.

Brazos waited and Mankin wolfishly watched the meat browning.

"Could you show us the way to the white man's camp?"

After a long time of just sitting, Mankin turned his shaggy head and looked sleepily at Brazos. "One of you. Just you— might take you there."

Brazos passed him the food and tried for patience. He waited a long time between questions, but it was soon apparent that they were getting nowhere.

"How far to the white man's camp?" Brazos asked again. Mankin stared at the fire a long time. "North. On the road." That was all. Brazos felt the tingling belief that here was something worth knowing, if he could dig it out. Teche had rolled in his blanket. Wid, Red, and Moss reclined nearby, smoking their pipes.

Brazos went into the darkness, rooting into his saddlebag. He returned clinking two gold coins and squatted across from Mankin. He played the coins in his fingers. A tiny curl of flame reflected on yellow gold. Mankin stared, then dropped his gaze to the coals.

There was no sound except the small flames and the coins clicking as Brazos scraped them back and forth.

Mankin muttered, "Topaz."

Brazos swore to himself. "Who is Topaz?"

Then it came in the old man's halting, half-jointed way of talking. Mankin had got word of a white man's camp and prisoners of the Indians from a Mexican wood hauler named Topaz, who had heard it from a Tonkawa squaw he kept in a dugout in the north post oak thickets, and she said that she was told it in a dream by a warrior's voice that rode the edge of the night wind. Teche called derisively from his bedding, "Maybe we better go hunting the damned night wind." Mankin packed his pipe bowl and picked a flaming twig from the fire. Brazos played the two gold pieces back and forth in his hands. Mankin did not look up again after one hungry glance. Then he took the pipe from his mouth and spoke without fully opening his half-closed eyes.

"There was men and buffalo wagons along the creek. Squaw might—could have heard there, instead of from the warrior's voice in her dream. Bad men—she would be afraid. She hid and heard talk."

"Might—could." Brazos clicked the gold pieces.

"Ugly man would cause a bad dream," Mankin said softly. "She was scared."

"How ugly, this man?"

"Hairy. All over. He has a name, up here."

Brazos stiffened, and sensed that Wid, Red, and Teche were straining to listen.

"Hairy like a *what?*"

Mankin faltered. Brazos jingled the coins.

"Like a *spider*." Mankin snarled.

Wid grunted a low oath behind him, and Brazos heard his own blood pumping fast in his ears. He felt his fingers moisten on the coins. He asked softly, "Would he be called a name like that? Like 'Spider'?"

Mankin showed the yellow fangs of a starved lobo caught

in a trap. "A bad one. Like he looks. Friend of Comanches. I've talked enough."

"Not yet. This buffalo wagon man—your squaw heard him speak to the Comanches?"

"Topaz's squaw, with the antelope ears. She heard and told my woman. The spider man—he knows about white prisoners north of Torrey's. Trades with Mexicans and Comanches."

"You can take me to the spider-man camp? Tonight, now?"

Mankin stiffened. "Might' near it. Show you where, over on the wagon trace. Now this is all I know." Mankin stretched his arm greedily and Brazos handed him the two coins.

Brazos told the others: "No time like now to find out if the Spider is up here to ambush us."

X

They rode through the black night until at last Mankin grunted for caution and halted his mule. "Camp's down there. Far as I'm goin'." As Brazos scrutinized the dark line of brush, Mankin vanished, man, mule and shadow.

Brazos tied his horse. He took out the saddle carbine, and began a cautious descent of the cedar-thick slope. He came to the rim of an arroyo and looked down and found the camp: one cat eye in the inky space below and a whisker of smoke. The fire was at the foot of the drop-off, not far below him, and he felt exposed, fearful that his sounds might have carried. Sound wouldn't have to be much, if they had an Indian lookout. If he spooked their *remuda* he'd bring the whole blasted camp out like a chunked bee log. The night stayed silent. He settled uneasily to wait for light enough to show him what the Spider might be up to and how many were in his party.

The night finally thinned and the camp took form. He found the outlines of a covered wagon, and the gravelike spacing of blankets. One of these soon came to life. A man got up and put wood on the coals. Now others floated erect and Brazos counted seven as the new flames gave them substance. Two long-haired Indians moved up to squat at the coals. Brazos' strained listening caught horse movements. Twisting, he saw the outlines of the horses on the same shelf where he lay. The worry plagued him. Where was their *remuda* lookout?

Then he stiffened, for Captain Spide had appeared at the fire. The Spider raised his shaggy head and stared hard across at the slope as if looking directly at Brazos' hiding place. He called out, a word or a name. An answering hail sounded at the *remuda*. Brazos swore silently; he had damned near blundered into the man on watch.

Before he could start his crawling retreat, the lookout walked very near. The man called in Spanish that he had heard a horse up the slope and was going to investigate.

Captain Spide then said something to the others and suddenly the fire glow played on emptiness. As Brazos watched, puzzled, one figure came out of the darkness and into the firelight. Brazos recognized the stooped shape of Trakken. He had no time to wonder at Trakken's presence. Where had the bunch vanished to? He studied the graying cut. Shadows moved across the bank. They were coming up. He squirmed backward through the cedars.

In thicker cover he stood and searched for the ridge above that marked his back trail. Before he realized it, he had walked into their scattered *remuda*. Horses plunged and fought their picket ropes. He backed off but the damage was done. A voice called, "Something's scaring the horses!"

The lookout emerged from the cedars almost upon him. As Brazos turned, a gunshot broke the dawn apart and a heavy club seemed to fan grazingly across the sleeve of his brush jacket. He plunged into the brush again and a second bullet rattled the branches. Sounds and movement seemed to come from all directions. He fought through the dark growth, desperately looking for his horse. He found an opening, headed fast for the far side and a shot crashed behind him. A yell drew an answering shot close to his right and he knew he was cut off from the animal. Better to lose the mustang than his own hide. He kept low and worked his way in silence again, this time to his left and upgrade from the thicket. Finally, with the sounds lost behind him, he bellied over a ridge, trotted down the other side, and plunged into mesquite brush again. He picked his way through the thorns to a rock-floored cut. For a long time he kept to the rocks that would leave no easily-followed sign, and when the sun lighted the eastern ridges he figured his directions and set a course. What he had to do was find the main valley down which the others had intended to move to the water hole Mankin had described. Then he would follow that valley north until he found their new camp, and water.

Through the long day he pushed on, keeping to concealment, avoiding the high ground. His thirst grew, and his hunger, and he had never known such weariness before. He lay in a weedy hollow at dusk and slept like a dead man. When he awoke, night blanketed the land and he was a lost particle in the dark maze, drifting ever north into the mesquite-choked gullies. Sometime in the night his foot sank in moist earth and he found a scummy water hole. He slept there until dawn, drank again, and got his bearings from the first sun streaks. At midday, while toiling through the brush of a meandering dry creek, he sighted a man ahead. He slipped into concealment behind a chalky upthrust and then made out the oncoming man as Teche.

Soon they faced each other, both drawn and red-eyed. Brazos forced a sour grin. "I botched it. But it's the Spider's outfit, set up for an ambush."

Teche flung off sweat. "You don't know what botchin' is, yet. Where's your horse?"

"Where's the camp? I'm damned thirsty."

"Down yonder apiece. We scattered out looking for sign of you. You been put afoot?"

More than ordinary anxiety sharpened Teche's tone. Brazos felt his face redden. "They jumped me. I was lucky to get out without my horse."

Teche chuckled harshly. "Welcome to the foot soldiers, then. The Indians hit us last night. We're *all* afoot!"

Brazos' first thought burst forth: "The gold?"

"Oh, it's safe enough. But not a horse to our name."

"Wid? Afoot in this?" It was too much to imagine.

"Yes, by God, Wid!"

Brazos sank to a rock and rubbed his dirt-caked stubble. The disaster was too big to take. Men were next to creeping death, caught in this country without horses. Brazos looked dismally at a high-up buzzard gliding with the heat currents.

"How did they do it?"

"Who knows how a damned Indian does it? All at once there they were, then they were gone, and we had no horses."

"Who was on watch?"

Teche squinted away at the far ugly country. "I was."

They sat for a while, silent. Brazos was not going to ask if Teche had fallen asleep while on sentry. He already knew the answer to that. Finally, Teche asked, "How much farther you figure to Torrey's?"

"What does Moss say?"

"He reckons we can walk it in two or three days."

Brazos stared at the endless stretch of ridges and thorny brush shimmering. "Not Wid. He can't walk it."

Teche headed down to the camp at the water hole. "He sure as hell will walk it now!"

To men afoot, the land quickly revealed its full, personal hatred against all invaders. A hundred body hurts and the thorny treacheries of the tangles plagued their walking in ways a man never noticed when up above it in a saddle. Just to see Wid fighting through the impeding mesquites and yuca spikes, up and down the eternal gullies, was enough to double the hurts of the others. When they first halted for a rest, each man sat where he stopped, put down his rifle and saddlebags, shook his canteen to his ear, and swallowed as little water from it as he could force himself to do with. Brazos sprawled beside Wid.

"You call out, Wid, whenever you feel you need a rest."

"Oh, it's not bad, old fellow. *He* had to walk the whole bloody distance to the City of Mexico. Now what about that Spider outfit?"

"They might be out to head us off. It may have to do with this money, or with the reason we're up here. The hide wagon makes 'em look like a buffalo outfit, but I have my doubts about that."

"Means we keep a sharp lookout from here to Torrey's," Wid commented. "Now, let's get going."

They hunted for a water hole in a shallow canyon in late afternoon. Getting to the bottom of the rocky grade was a chore for Wid. "The damned stump. Like it'd been stuck in a fire."

Moss said, "We could fashion a stretcher, brought my blanket roll just for that purpose, in case—"

"Oh, hell, Moss, I can walk! Just steady me a little."

"Dry as a bone!" Teche called. They looked at the crusted mud. Teche and Brazos wasted an hour in a fruitless search of the canyon. By the time they gave up all the canteens were nearly dry.

In the brush again, they strung out and bent to the endless plodding. Mesquite thickets, prickly pear clumps as high as horses, and rank stretches of dagger-sharp bear grass had to be penetrated or circled. Wid fell farther behind. Red Myrick began to stagger, weak with fever. Brazos, Teche, and Moss made alternate swings out from their line of march, struggling to higher ground to scan their back trail and the country. When they passed near each other once, exchanging places for the lookout, Brazos and Teche traded glances and Brazos saw a thin mocking smile flicker on Teche's dust-caked mouth.

Teche murmured, "You look like you've just waltzed through a pack of Comanche squaws."

Brazos felt his thorn cuts and muscle hurts boil up in scalding resentment, but he controlled himself because nobody else had said a word about Teche's going to sleep and losing their horses. They never had been a family to speak blame in a bad fix, so he wasn't going to start now. The grin, as if sparked by some secret humor, died off Teche's face. "You know we can't do more than one more day of this, don't you?"

Brazos glanced to the back trail. "You think he's about finished?"

"Every step tomorrow will be like he's got a hot sword running through that knee. On top of that, Red Myrick's wobbly from dengue fever or something. Who knows when we'll find water again, if ever?"

Brazos knuckled at the sweat and bloody scratches on his face. "We've got to have horses."

"Part of us could hole up," said Teche. "Two of us, say, keep walking till we found Torrey's, then manage some mustangs to bring in the others."

"There's another out. If we sight smoke of a camp at sundown, it will mean horses and water. You above night rustling?"

"From your friend, the Spider?"

"If we can locate his camp. He's moving toward Torrey's over there on the wagon trace. There'd be an Indian or Mexican wrangler to handle. You know that."

Teche touched his belt knife. "I'm thirsty and tired of walking."

"It all depends if we sight camp smoke. Teche, damn it —how'd it happen?"

He saw the lift of Teche's eyebrow and the irony of his glance. "Why now, brother, a thing will just happen. You lost a horse yourself, remember. Happens to the best of us."

"I wasn't asleep when I lost mine!" Brazos retorted.

Teche chuckled. "You know how I hate explanations."

They camped where the brush was thickest. Canteens that had a slosh left in them were passed and each man wet his mouth. At sundown, Brazos watched from the high rim and found a far-off wisp of smoke. Too far to go there and back tonight. Tomorrow they could angle their course to close the distance. He studied the intervening roughs in the dusk, figuring the route they would have to take, the cover they could expect. Then he went down to the others and told what he had seen. "Teche and I will make a scout up that way tomorrow night, if we're close enough to do it."

"The Spider, you think?" Moss asked.

"Could be. Or it might be a Cherokee bunch."

"You got horses in mind?"

"We could buy 'em if it's a friendly tribe or a white outfit. Steal 'em if they're not."

Red Myrick was stretched with a thorn-bloodied arm across his face. He groaned. "Don't be bringing the whole Spider pack down on us. Doubt I could run."

Moss muttered, "You got the dengue. When a man's got that, he just never wants to get on his feet again."

Night closed down to hide each man and his hurts. Hunger drove them to chew on dried meat and cold *penole* bread from saddlebags, food that was more unpalatable than ever because of thirst-parched tongues. They struggled out of blanket rolls in the first dawn light. Red Myrick said that he doubted if he could stand, much less walk. Moss touched an empty canteen to his mouth. He took it down and said wryly, "I thought it might have dewed a little in there."

Wid was off to one side, doing his stump-wrapping in private. "That's nothing, Red," he called gruffly. "You ought to try rubbing a hurtin' leg that's not here." Brazos walked over, braving Wid's sensitive, belligerent glance that told him to stay away. He got a look at the exposed stump. In the pink scarred skin ridges of Wid's knee he saw a maze of tiny black blisters looking like a nest of dead ants. Wid finished rubbing on grease and got busy with the cloth wrapping and leather harness.

Brazos went back and draped his gear over him. Bag, rifle, and canteen. A ton each. Wid hobbled up, his red-streaked eyes working everywhere. He spat fluffy cotton, "Come on, Red—run you a race!" Brazos' eyes misted and he cursed under his breath.

They toiled through the mesquites, cactus, and cedars. It helped Brazos a little, thinking how it might have been for Seale in shackles with bayonets pushing him all the way to Perote Prison. But the hurts, thirst, and thorns were still there.

They always came back. The September sun fried out his skin and he tasted dust when there wasn't any dust, and tried to swallow saliva when there was none of that either. When Teche went upgrade to scout their line of march, Brazos felt such bitterness against him for getting them into this plight, that he turned the other way. He dropped back to walk beside Wid.

As if he might have read Brazos' feeling, Wid talked, a few words at a time, fighting shortness of breath. "Teche wouldn't tell you in a week. Stubborn. You think he went to sleep on watch the other night and lost our horses. Well, it wasn't that. So get it out of your craw."

"You mean the redskins stole the horses with him wide awake?"

"Now cool your blasted gun, boy. Teche sure as hell was wide awake. What's more, he waded right in and fought the best he could. You'd have seen two dead Comanches in the brush if you'd looked, and also you might notice where Teche took an arrow through the skin of his britches leg. It was the rest of us being too slow getting there, that's where the blame lays if you're looking for blame. They faded off like a fog, our horses with 'em, and Teche carrying on a one-man chase, but the damage was done."

Guiltily, Brazos remembered Teche's wry comment about how he hated to make explanations. That was like Teche. In his stunned anger over the disaster he had been too quick to assume that Teche had gone to sleep on watch. Wid gave him a knowing sidewise grimace. Before Brazos could say anything, they came upon Red Myrick hunkered down in the grass. Red raised weak eyes and shook his head.

"Take it easy, Red," said Wid. "I'll join you for a minute." He lowered himself beside Red. Brazos looked at both of them where they sprawled with their consuming sufferings. Teche limped down from the brush ridge. Meeting him, Brazos, asked, "How's the arrow wound, Teche?"

Teche shrugged. "What's happened back there? They all in?"

"You did well, bagging two of the Indians. One man can't do much about it when a whole band hits the horses in the dark." The apology was there. Brazos added sheepishly, "If I hadn't been so spooked by the Spider's bunch I'd have found my own horse. Then we'd at least have had a mount for Wid." He hoped that made up for what he had wrongly thought about his brother.

"Ah, too much Risa Driscoll on your mind, old fellow."
Teche twisted his mouth in a sardonic grin. Brazos bristled.
Teche chuckled and changed hands with his rifle to wipe his
sweaty palms. "And speaking of old friends, I think tonight
is our night. I spotted some dust just now. Not far off. Your
Spider outfit, maybe, over on the wagon trail. If so, they're
looking for us, and by God we're looking for them—a little
nocturnal horse transaction, I mean. You in good strength?"

"Never better. I'm ready if you are."

Moss came back to see what the delay was, and they
turned it into a council of war. At last, Wid said, "You two
plan it the way you think best. It's a cinch Red and I can't
help any. Just get back with your own skins, that's all I say.
Horses, too, if possible!"

Moss added, "And all the water you can carry."

They decided to hole up where they were while Brazos
and Teche made their try. Another scout for a water hole
proved futile. Brazos and Teche worked their way to the
top of the mound at sunset and watched the brush line to
the northeast until a smoke smear showed itself.

Brazos said, "Let's move. Take us till midnight to get
there."

XI

Trakken brought food from the cookfire to the disheveled
girl in the wagon.

They no longer tied her hands; the welts on her wrists
were almost healed. During the lonely hours within her small
world of wagonbed captivity, Risa's mind had woven one
improbable escape plan after another. Once she had tried to
slip forward and grab the gun from the burly halfbreed
driver, and had been cuffed with a bruising palm for her
effort.

Trakken told her that dissension was growing among Captain Spide's crew. For the past two days she had observed
that Trakken himself had grown nervous and afraid.

"Some of the men want to set you afoot out here," Trakken said in a low voice. "The Spider says there's a better
use for you, for getting the McClouds in a trap if the ambush fails. You would be bait. I am afraid for you." He
added hoarsely, "And for myself. I thought I was getting
documents for the English and got caught in a trap. A vile

Mexican trap. This bunch is the main contact between Santa Anna and the tribes."

Risa asked urgently, "What are they intending to do, Trakken?"

The haggard man answered slowly. "Captain Spide knows that Seale McCloud can identify him as the one who handled the prisoner trade and he will never let McCloud go free. I have the feeling in my bones that all of us who know Captain Spide's part in what the Mexicans have done will never live to tell about it."

"Couldn't we get to the horses sometime in the night?"

"We wouldn't get far."

"We could try!" Risa urged. "What would we have to lose? Let's go tonight! If we can only get two horses, just a little start—"

"The sentries are very watchful since that trouble the other night. The Spider is not sure if the horse they found belonged to a stray somebody up here, or one of the McClouds. The men are also afraid that the Rangers may show up before they reach their Indian contact at the far end of the Valle de Cuchillos. But—I will see."

When the camp settled to sleep, Risa stayed wide awake. She prayed that Trakken would come, that this would be the night. She tossed fitfully in her tangled blankets. Could it have been the McClouds who created the disturbance the other night? Perhaps Brazos himself? But no, she was indulging in fantasies. Likely the McClouds would never wish to see her again because her father had failed them in delivery of the documents. She listened to the sound of the horses, the changing of the sentries. After long hours she heard the crunch of a footstep at the wagon and Trakken's voice.

"You should get out and—go to the bushes, now—like—just natural."

Struggling across the wagon gear, she slid over the tailgate. In the shadowy starlight she walked upright to the bushes near the picketed horses. The Mexican sentry on watch chuckled and bobbed his rifle and did not try to look away. Across the screening brush she heard Trakken speaking conversationally and the guard's amused reference to her.

Words ended in a thud, a grunt, the sound of a falling body. Risa caught her breath. Trakken called urgently. She ran to him, seeing Trakken straighten from the sentry's prone form in the weeds. He wiped his pistol on his pants leg.

"Very quiet, now!"

Time dragged for her while Trakken brought over saddles and bridles. Her heart was pounding in anxiety as they mounted. In the same moment, all the mustangs began fighting their ropes. Her nerves screamed in an agony of panic, but she forced herself to hold her horse to a walk as Trakken was doing. She called to Trakken, asking him please to ride faster. The yell behind them almost shattered her last clutch at control. The sentry had not been unconscious for long. She heard voices raised at the camp. Trakken said, "Now, *ride!*" She slapped the reins against the pony's hide, the night wind rang in her ears, the mesquite branches slapped her face. She held on and desperately followed Trakken into the darkness.

Brazos and Teche found the stream of water first and relieved their burning thirst. Now they fixed the location of the *remuda* in the thicket and the sleeping camp downgrade toward the cut. All they could do, for a little while, was to stretch exhausted. The walk in the night, the whole day's struggle, had taken too much out of them, Brazos thought. They could never make a fight of it. They lay for a long time in the low brush, getting their wind, watching the outline of the sentry. This time there must be no mistake.

Teche's mouth came almost against his ear. "Well, you ready?"

"Get the horses, I'll take care of the sentry."

His fingers locked on the Colt grip. Teche began inching away. Brazos started toward the dark outline of the guard.

Then he came to a dead stop and knew Teche had stopped, too. He felt a sickening surge of disappointment as he saw the shadow of another man join the guard.

He heard a Mexican voice, and the name, "Trakken." Fragments of talk. The Mexican said something about a girl.

The next he knew, Teche was gripping his arm and they were staring through the leafy screen at an almost soundless action. One dark form raised his arm, steel cracked on a skull, one man went down. The figure of a woman, skirts swishing, ran toward the horses. In another minute the two showed again as bent shadows riding through the mesquite bushes. The *remuda* began fighting picket ropes.

Teche breathed, "My God! You see that?"

"Quick! Grab a horse before the whole camp explodes!"

They took saddles and bridles out of the gear line, stumbling too noisily, Brazos knew, in their hurry. The lookout came to life. He struggled half erect and split the night with a yell. Brazos rode him down, swinging his Colt barrel solidly against the side of his upraised head, and once again the sentry crumpled.

They rode through the thicket, leaving the camp sounds dying behind them, setting a false trail north. Later, they circled back to the southwest, crossing the creek again and stopping to fill two canteens.

Teche commented, "Well, we pulled it. But what was all the charades, you think? Man and woman rode out ahead of us, sure as hell."

"Looked that way to me," Brazos agreed. "The man clubbed the sentry, then the two of them took off. One of the Spider's men and the camp *puta*, I reckon."

At dawn they reached the hidden camp. Moss Dean came out of the cedars to meet them. Teche handed him a canteen. "Drink up, Uncle. How's Wid?"

"You ain't a second too soon," Moss said glumly. He jerked a thumb. "Look yonder."

Brazos saw Wid sitting on a boulder, his big shoulders slumped, his tortured stump showing red in the dawn. The leather rigging and peg lay on the ground. Wid was staring off into space as Brazos hurried over with a canteen. Wid moved his head slowly and Brazos saw the glassy cast to his stare.

"You keep 'em from annexing Texas, son, you do that," Wid said in a far-off voice. Brazos shot a look at his uncle. Moss nodded bleakly. "Infection, I think. He's half out of his head."

Brazos put his arm around Wid's shoulders and tilted the canteen to the dust-caked mouth. Wid's skin was hot to his touch. Afterward, he saw Wid fall back and close his eyes and heard his labored breathing.

Moss said, "Red's down there, and not much better off than Wid."

Brazos rubbed his jaw and looked back at Wid's prone body. Nothing would be any good if anything happened to Wid.

"I'll take him in to Torrey's," Brazos said. "You help me get him on one of these horses, then you two and Red hole up around here somewhere till I send horses out. Suit you?"

"Go ahead," said Moss. "Just hope to God somebody at

Torrey's knows a little doctorin'. Watch out for the Spider's outfit on the way. But if you make it, you can trust Bartolo, I think."

Teche helped him load Wid into the saddle, with his knee leather and wooden leg strapped back into place, and Brazos was heartened to see Wid make a weak grin of understanding. They rode to the ridge and Brazos got his bearings, while the three left behind vanished to hole up in the brush with their hurts and hunger.

Once during the ride through the rocky arroyos and cactus thickets, Brazos caught sight of a far-off dust trace toward the wagon route. Captain Spide traveling? He hoped they had lost any trail sign he and Teche might have left. The dust drifted south of west in a direction that would miss Torrey's. This was puzzling. It looked as if Captain Spide might be meaning to bypass the settlement. If so, what would be his destination and purpose? To waylay the McClouds somewhere beyond? Could mean that the Spider would know where they would go from Torrey's to make their contact. Uneasily, he rode down to rejoin Wid. His brother pointed and said thickly, "Yonder's the foot of the Valle de Cuchillos. You be sure we swing well north of that mess."

"Don't worry. We'll follow the Concho."

They circled the great tangled sweeps of the dagger-bristling ocean of desolation that was the impenetrable Valley of Knives. Brazos led the way along a crusted rock plateau and soon located the line of greener growth that marked the Concho. Just before dusk, they looked upon the handful of shacks and tents above the river.

Brazos tasted this arrival like a peppery meal long smelled by a hungry man. Here, at last, was a goal reached, a goal hard come by, the jumping-off place for whatever lay beyond, for the answer to the fate of Seale McCloud. Here was where a man had to come to start. If there were white prisoners to the north, word of gold and a trade ready to be made could fly both ways from Torrey's on the invisible wings of prairie whispers mysteriously relayed.

He turned back to the slumped, sick figure of Wid and pointed to the scattering of huts on the catclaw flat above the coiling course of the pitiful little desert river. "There it is, Wid. Torrey's Post!"

They rode into Torrey's as the sun went down, two cautious articles of dirty drift off a dirty country, two watchful strangers with the feel of curious eyes on them. They rode their stolen horses through a sun-dried straggle of Cherokee tepees, wickiups, and mud-plastered shacks, toward the largest adobe buildings and horse pens. Three ancient trade wagons stood empty and bleached in the broomweeds.

The low-topped 'dobe had a long, brush-awning porch. Brazos saw on the roof corners the ready snouts of the two cannons like crouched death ready to spring upon the distant brush. Rumor said the main reasons why Torrey's was strangely immune from Indian attack were the loaded cannons and Bartolo's reputation.

Wid murmured, "Town wasn't bred for beauty, was it?"

"You keep a sharp watchout, now," Brazos cautioned. He was looking everywhere, on the off chance the Spider's outfit might have pulled in ahead of them. He dismounted at the porch. A stocky Mexican looked them over. Without waiting to be told, he helped Brazos slide Wid from the saddle and steady him up the steps and into the building.

Brazos searched through the jumble of trade goods and hide stacks, until he sighted the long-haired man who sat watching them from a rocking chair.

The long-haired man got up and came toward them in his own good time. He was wrinkled and browned by both sun and breeding, wearing a blanket coat and moccasins. His shrewd ageless face indicated Indian and white mixing, and he seemed to be speculating on their thorn-torn clothing, all the cuts and dirt and hunger from the hard trail, and the exact nature and weight of the contents of the bag that Brazos carried.

"I'm Brazos McCloud. My brother, Wid. You're Bartolo, I suppose."

Without turning, Bartolo spoke to the Mexican who brought a whisky bottle out of the gloom while Brazos assisted Wid to a seat on a wood bench. Bartolo said in English: "You look needful of this."

The whisky burned pleasingly against the trail grit and pain. Wid adjusted his wooden leg and wiped his fever-cracked mouth. "Place's a little hard gettin' to, Bartolo."

"You're Seale McCloud's sons. Money on you, looking for your *padre*."

"How'd you know that?"

"News has a way of blowing in here with the dust."

The shaggy trader, when he spoke, revealed a kind of dignity, a mixture of strength and aloofness. Brazos felt in his presence the force that ruled this last outpost. Here was the legendary trader who held the confidence alike of Indians, Mexican raiders, and the Austin government.

"First off," said Brazos, "we expect trouble from a trail outfit run by Captain Spide. I'd like to know what to look for from you, if they come in here. Next, and pretty damned fast, my brother needs some medicine and doctoring—"

Bartolo studied Wid. "Heard rumors of you. Keep my little army ranging a way. There'll be no violence tolerated from Captain Spide or anybody else in this settlement. As for doctoring, we'd first better bed you. There's an empty shack you can quarter in. You may have a long wait." He spoke to the Mexican who padded out. "There's a part-Indian woman here, widow named Willow. She's nearest thing we've got to somebody who can doctor a sick man. Now, where's the rest of your party?"

"Maybe I'd better tell you our whole story." Then Brazos related it, the McCloud mission, the loss of their horses, his belief that Spide planned an ambush somewhere beyond, the burning question of whether Seale might be a captive at the upper stretches of Valle de Cuchillos.

Bartolo looked off into the distance. "Everything takes patience. It has been done before. Ransom has been passed and the prisoners were brought in. Gold does it. Your job now is to get word to the right chief."

Wid demanded, "Is Seale McCloud out there or not? How straight have you heard about that?"

"Heard! Heard! Thing here is to sort the chaff of all you hear and decide how much truth you've got. Yes, I've heard he's a prisoner. That's all I can tell you."

"About Captain Spide," Brazos put in. "Does he come here?"

"He trades out of here once in a while," Bartolo said shortly. He changed the subject. "You will wait here in the settlement. One night, word will drift in like a lost buzzard and you will know how to proceed. That's all I can tell you for the moment. Horses for the rest of your party, yes. I will send a man to pick them up.

"Your father and your uncle are known to me by reputation."

XII

A black-haired woman of Wid's age came to the shack with food, candles, and medicine. Wid, on his blanket pallet, at first resisted with fevered belligerence her effort to uncover his leg stump.

"No woman looks at that ugly mess!"

"Whatever it is, I've seen worse," said Willow quietly. "I survived the Llano massacre and saw what happened to my husband and all the other men."

"Let her doctor you!" Brazos commanded. "Don't be so McCloud stubborn! You're in a bad state—"

Wid relented to the gentle but sure way she went about bathing the inflamed flesh. When Brazos left them to explore the settlement, Wid appeared fully resigned to Willow's work with carbolic, quinine, and herb water.

From the first night on, waiting idly was the worst of it for Brazos. Bartolo's post force of tame Cherokees, half-breeds, and Mexicans drifted in and out of the settlement. They evaded his efforts to make talk. Bartolo was aloof when Brazos saw him again in the headquarters building. The day dragged by. He spent most of the time in the shack with Wid. Trouble was, he didn't know what to expect here, when word would come, or how, or what they would be told to do. There was nothing but mystery out in the purple simmer of September heat over the frowning badlands and brush.

Willow returned to administer to Wid. She said his fever was broken, and that his stump infection was healing. Wid by now had come to accept her attention, even detaining her with talk when she was ready to leave. Willow was graceful in movement, soft-eyed and quiet spoken. Brazos mentioned that she was a good-looking woman. Wid murmured, "And a damned smart one. Indians killed her husband, years back, and she kept living here at the post. She told me all about it."

On the afternoon of the third day the rest of the party rode in from the south. One of Bartolo's settlement Cherokees led the procession up to the shack. Red Myrick hung to his saddle horn in the helpless way of a man wracked with dengue and weakness. They bedded him alongside Wid and the Cherokee went to find Willow, while Brazos brought Teche and Moss up to date on the situation in Torrey's.

Moss commented: "Well, it's about like I thought it'd be.

We get here and we wait for word to drift in. Bartolo will show no help one way or the other, but he's foxy. Doing more than it looks like. He stands in with all sides, and that ain't as bad as it sounds. It's the way he manages to keep ahold of the situation up here. All sides know he's to be trusted. And those two cannons on the roof have got the bad tribes buffaloed. They hate the big-noise guns."

"What do we do when word comes?" Teche wanted to know. "Just three of us able-bodied enough to ride out yonder for the contact. How do we know we won't lose the gold and our scalps as well in some kind of trap? This damn place is a tricky one, way I see it, and I include Bartolo."

"He's all we've got to go on," Brazos argued. "What else can we do but wait?"

"While Bartolo frames up something with the Spider?" retorted Teche with sarcasm.

"I doubt that," grunted Moss. "We can do worse, Teche, than rest up and get some food in us, and our second wind. God knows what we got to tackle when time comes to hit Valle de Cuchillos."

Teche was not satisfied, but he had no answer. Brazos, like Teche, chaffed under the strain of inaction, the beat of impatience against delay. That night, the first message came.

Starlight showed at the doorless opening. Brazos felt a presence and sat upright, his hand closing on his Colt. Teche moved, too, and Moss stood with pistol raised. All stared intently at the opening. The figure there showed full length against the night sky. Moccasins whispered on the clay floor.

"Stand your tracks!" Moss ordered. "Three guns on you."

"Don't shoot, *señor*." The man stood still. "Please do not show a light. I have been asked to say to you, go to the Valle de Cuchillos."

Brazos asked, "Where? What part of the Valle?"

"The north rim. Follow it, and you will be told. . . ."

The shadow flowed out into the night. Hastening to the doorway, they scanned the darkness. Nothing moved that they could see except the mesquite branches swaying among the distant dark shacks.

Soon after dawn they told Bartolo of their visitor, but nothing registered in his granite face. "I am unable to advise you. You have their first message. What more do you want?"

"We have to agree to that," Moss admitted. "Can we borrow horses again?"

Bartolo said, "Of course." And that was all they could get out of him. Brazos felt the rebuff. The procedure was so vague as to make him feel frustrated, then angry. Yet, he concluded that there might have been hidden meaning in Bartolo's words. Wasn't he telling them to act, now, to start for the Valley of Knives? Somewhere out there, Bartolo might have been saying, more information would be passed. "One thing," Brazos finally said, "the gold—do we take it this time?"

Bartolo asked pointedly, "Were you told to?"

Brazos admitted, "No."

"Then you have answered your own question."

Later, when Willow had visited the sick pair and departed, Red Myrick watched the preparations of the three to ride for the brush. "You're not leavin' me behind," he protested. "Feel able to hit it, now. Just wait—"

"Nope," Moss growled. "You got a job right here, Red. You sit over this gold with a cocked gun in your hand. Also, somebody needs to stay with Wid."

Teche joshed, "Aw, Wid's got another nurse he likes better. The slinky good-looker, Willow—"

Wid bristled, growling an embarrassed oath at Teche. Red gave up his argument. Brazos, Teche, and Moss rode from the settlement on their borrowed mustangs.

The shacks quickly vanished in the brushy distance behind them. They climbed steadily for two hours, up the stair steps of rocky layers of desert growth, then parallel to the thorn jungle of the Cuchillos, westward along its northern rim. Here was a high lost world of primitive red crags and catclaw crevices, tortuously bordering the green spikes and cactus monsters in the tangle below. Made to order, thought Brazos, for an ambush. Their eyes searched constantly ahead, to all sides. The Spider's crew or the Comanches from the north could strike instantly, popping up from the earth at their feet. When a man came face to face with the country, its wildness and resentment, thought Brazos, he would marvel at his one-time eagerness to come north and tackle it. It had been an age ago, it seemed, since they had left civilization. San Antonio, the McCloud homestead, the girls, his bold journey into Louisiana to rob a United States messenger, these seemed fragments of a lost time. Dwarfed by the boulders, the thorny brush, the dropoff into the sword-bristling valley, a man found it hard to care any longer what happened to the Texas government, so far behind him.

Or the fate of government documents. Even the memory of Risa Driscoll faded into a realm unrelated to the present.

Then he drew up his horse so suddenly that Moss and Teche quickly lifted their rifles and started looking for whatever he had seen. But this was something in a suddenly opened recess of his memory.

"No, by God!" Brazos muttered aloud. That voice the other night. When he and Teche were stalking the Spider's *remuda* lookout. *The girl on the horse.* The few low Spanish words she had said to Trakken as the two fled. It hadn't dented his memory under stress of that moment. But it came back now, staggering him. Those few words she had spoken were in Spanish, and in an undertone, words having only to do with making haste. The substance of them he barely remembered. But what came back now was the inflection. That Spanish she had spoken had been with a *British accent!*

No girl of Spanish blood he'd ever heard speak had a funny little English clip to soft Spanish, except Risa.

"What's the trouble?" Teche demanded, looking everywhere.

"Nothing," Brazos muttered.

"You looked spooked," Moss rasped. "Lemme take the lead."

He *was* spooked. The association was too preposterous to deserve thinking about. But now the size of the shadow that night fitted his recollections, and the intangible movement of her, and most of all, those few low words to Trakken. He let the other two pass him on the trail, and shook his head hard to jar sense back. The strain was getting him, he guessed. Instead of Red's dengue or Wid's blood infection, he was having something worse. Hallucinations.

Moss held his hand high and halted. Their three rifles settled. A swarthy man in old buckskins who sat a skittish Indian pony rode from behind a mesquite mound dead ahead and sat squinting intently at their approach.

"This is a friendly meeting, *señores.* I am here with a message from people unknown to me. Do you wish to hear it?"

"Keep talking," Moss said.

"There is a place you will wish to go." He unbent two fingers. "This many hours ride from here on the same rim of the Cuchillos. A red stone cliff of double spires. A place you are to wait."

"What time, *amigo?*" asked Brazos.

The man showed four fingers. "These many nights from now."

"We must wait that long?"

"*Sí*. And bring the gold."

"You know our mission?" Teche demanded. "You know who we are?"

"Please, *señor*. I am only a poor rider who happened this way."

"Speak up, man!" Teche flourished his gun. "Who the hell sent you? Give us some proof."

That was going to be all. The man was turning his pony. Moss muttered to Teche to calm down. There was no reason to detain the old Spaniard and in a moment he had vanished behind the crags like a ghost who'd never been there at all. Brazos looked down upon the ugly, shimmering valley of bristling cactus, mesquites, and yucca daggers. Far to the northwest went the jagged line of red cliffs that marked the land's turmoil until the plains set in above the Caprock. Comanche country, from the cliffs on. Four nights from now? They talked it over. Thing to do was go back to Torrey's, get the gold, outfit themselves for a long stay in the wilds, and return to keep the rendezvous. With one extra horse for Seale. By then, perhaps Wid and Red would be able to ride with them.

Teche remarked, "Anybody thinking what I am? That maybe this breed was a decoy? Way to get us and the gold for your spy friend, the Spider?"

Moss grunted something noncommittal and turned for the back trail. Teche followed him. Brazos brought up the rear. The two ahead soon went out of his sight where the route twisted between shoulders of redstone and brush. The tail of his eye caught a flutter of something down the cliffside to his right. Jack rabbit, maybe, or cougar. But he thought he'd seen a flash of bright colors in the rocks and mesquites toward the Valley of Daggers. He worked his horse through the rocks and head-high catclaw of the descent, his rifle ready, trying to mark the place in the brushy tangle that had caught his eye. He thought once to yell to the others to wait, but this probably would turn into something inconsequential and they would be chaffed at the delay.

The movement showed again and it was no jack rabbit. Brazos cocked his rifle, warily nudging the horse ahead. Human movement, he now felt certain. He wished that Teche and Moss had not gone so far ahead of him.

"Come out of there!" he called.

His rifle held on the gnarled cedars. Two figures moved out like bedraggled growth from the arid ground. Brazos sat with his rifle barrel becoming a shaking twig. He looked in numbness at the haggard, ragged figure of Trakken. And the girl. The stumbling girl with dark tangled hair, the small feminine body in the torn calico that swam like a heat mirage to his vision. Her eyes held to him. The gladness that flowed into them made tears glisten on her lashes. A thankful cry burst from her throat. He mumbled more with his brain than with his tongue: "Risa!"

She ran toward him and stumbled in the rocks. He got down and walked to her. She sat where she had fallen and wiped her eyes.

Trakken began blabbering. "By God, man, we thought we were done for. Can you get us out of here? The Spider and his bunch are somewhere around and hard after us."

XIII

Trouble was, a man could wander off a few rods and be lost in this wild tangle. Why the hell hadn't Moss and Teche waited, or come back to look for him?

Trakken stumbled along, gushing out the story of their flight. Brazos had put Risa on his horse to follow his and Trakken's slow uphill walk through scrub growth and boulders. He carried the rifle.

"Had to leave our horses two days ago," Trakken puffed. "No water. They cut us off from Torrey's, kept crowding us toward that cactus jungle down there. We hid out by day, walked at night. Sometimes they were nearly on us. You hear me, McCloud! They're somewhere around! No telling how close—"

"I hear you. So will the bunch chasing you if you don't quiet down." By now he'd had the gist of the whole thing. How Driscoll had been trapped in San Antonio, the kidnaping of Risa, the Spider's work for Mexico, and his plan to ambush the McClouds northwest of Torrey's before they made contact with their father's captors. Hearing all this had made the delay longer, but he'd had to wait for the pair of them to get their wind and sip on his canteen.

He struggled on, hunting for an opening where he might see a little of the land eastward. Surely his uncle and brother would have turned back by now. He gained the rim and soon found the hoof tracks. Then, farther along, he was startled to see many new tracks mix with those of Moss's and Teche's horses. He brought his rifle around, listening, frowning at Trakken for silence. Couldn't be but one reason they had not come back to look for him. Moss and Teche were in trouble somewhere in the tangle beyond the next rocky pinnacles.

"Keep your pistol ready. Stay with Risa."

He slipped into the cedars and worked through to a massive upthrust of gray rocks. Edging around these, he gained a view east across a bristling patch of giant yucca swords.

There the trouble was, spread out against a red rock cliff like a grisly saloon painting he had once seen of a Spanish execution the way a town artist had imagined it. He saw Teche and Moss standing against the bare flat cliff face, arms raised, just their backs showing to the dark-hued, silent men clustered behind them. Brazos recognized Captain Spide and knew that death was just a few seconds away from Moss and Teche. They had been ambushed and disarmed. Obviously, it had happened so quickly that they never had a chance to fight. It was plain that the Spider's hunt for Trakken and Risa had been side-tracked here on the rim of the Cuchillos for an ambush of a different set of victims. He was having Moss and Teche executed on the spot with bullets in their backs.

The range was far but time was racing. Brazos forcibly closed his mind to shut out tension, concentrating only on the aim that had to be perfect. He made his rifle sight hold thin and still, let a breath of pent-up air ease from his lungs. The sight stayed engraved on the upper body of the nearer of the two-man firing squad. He tightened on the trigger so slowly that his gun jerked and roared as if firing itself. Teche's would-be executioner, a long-haired breed, pitched his rifle straight up and staggered in a circle to a wilting fall. The other rifleman, who had been raising his gun on Moss, half turned, mystified, to gape at his companion's antics. Brazos loaded, took a new bead, and shot this one. The rest of the painting began to run its colors, coming apart in a mess of rearing horses, churned red dust and confused voices, with Teche and Moss running. Brazos yelled to them, "Get to your horses!"

The two of them reached their ponies. He saw that their rifle boots were empty. The Spider and the others who had been mounted had spurred into the brush. Shooting sounded out of his vision. The rifle in his hand jolted as a slug crashed steel and a splinter nicked his ear. A bullet splashed yucca fragments over him and he dodged back to the cedars, seeing his rifle was cracked and useless. Trakken floundered through the brush. Risa was fighting the horse upgrade and Brazos called to her, gesturing toward Teche and Moss, and saw her circle to join them. She barely made it to the mesquites where those two were piling on their mustangs. Two riders charged out of the tangle to Brazos' left with rifles booming. He fired his Colt, missed, and plunged for new cover with Trakken at his heels. He got a final glimpse of the fleeing and unarmed trio, Moss, Teche, and Risa, riding quickly out of his sight. The Spider's force had cut off Trakken and him from the others. Slugs began chipping the rock shielding his position. He could sight no clear target, and they were stalking down on him, spread for the kill. He had no choice but to keep retreating downgrade. Trakken crawled with him, eyes yellow with panic. Brazos heard the far-off retreating sounds of Moss, Teche, and Risa. The last crackle of their escape run died out toward the back trail and Torrey's. "By God, they made it!" he kept saying.

Afoot, rifle gone, Trakken on his hands, he put down a momentary feeling of abandonment. Only thing those three could do—head for Torrey's. Moss and Teche had lost their guns and were helpless to do anything for him. And they had Risa to get to safety.

He heard the Spider's riders calling back and forth, out of sight. He thought that the wily Spider would be quick to guess that this was Brazos who had broken up his bushwhack of Moss and Teche, that he was now cut off from the others and cornered, and that where Brazos was the gold likely would be.

He said to Trakken, "We can get out of this if you can take a little blood-letting." He motioned toward the dark sea of giant spikes. "We cross over."

Trakken gasped. "That's suicide!"

"They've got us cut off above."

Trakken twisted for a frightened look at the Cuchillos in the nearly vertical dropoff below. "Not into *that!*"

"It's our only way out of here."

Bullets splashed the brush over their heads from three directions. Trakken groaned like a dying man. Brazos waited no longer. In a sliding fall he went down the crumbling rock ledge, Trakken close upon him. They descended crashing and rolling down the loose rocks and catclaw slope. First they hit the tangle of skin-stabbing yucca on the fringes and it was like falling into a mass of angry bees. They struggled deeper into the maze of bayonet trees.

Shielding his eyes and face with upraised arms, head and body bent low, Brazos struggled sideways into the Valle de Cuchillos. Every bristling, living bayonet in the mile-wide valley, every crowded colony of prickly pear, Spanish dagger, rattlesnake and Gila monster seemed to flash the vindictive signal ahead that here was human blood for tasting.

The bear grass grew taller than his head and choking thick, with rigid needle-sharp spikes reaching to pierce any moving thing. Interspersed with it were ancient prickly pear clumps in grotesque shapes waiting to brush a plaster of needles at the slightest touch of bare skin or clothing. Where was any opening for a man's body? Brazos wavered in hopelessness.

The thorns and spikes seemed impenetrable. No way to go on without a man stabbing himself in a hundred places. But the gunfire kept up from the ridge. They had him spotted from up there.

Crawling low to the ground, he found that he could make slow progress below the worst of the spikes. The floor beneath the overhead maze of green and brown stilettos was mostly flinty rocks and dwarf prickly pear. Punishment enough, but a man crawled or got punctured to death by the spikes above. Fighting off panic from the trapped feeling was the thing. The wild obsession was to rise, fight it, run. Apaches couldn't have devised anything worse. Trapped and smothering, covered with wounds, and oozing blood, Brazos felt near madness. He had to take his will in his fist and make himself stay down.

He heard Trakken struggling and moaning behind him. Bullets poured in from the distant ledge, sprinkling green pulp. Thing to do was never look up. He crawled with his body dragging the flint stones and ground thorns, steeled against visioning what waited just inches above. A rattlesnake slid out of the litter of dead stuff in the dried cactus bottoms immediately ahead.

Brazos stopped and pulled out his Colt. This movement sent the rattler into a businesslike fat coil in his path. At that point Brazos saw that he was hemmed in by prickly

pear on both sides of his crowded tunnel and that the rattler eyed him with flat head upraised as if it meant to
spend the day.

"Hold it, Trakken. Back up a little."

He heard Trakken struggle to turn, which was a mistake.
He should have slid backward in the tight space. Trakken
cursed from a new rash of spike stabs. Then, unable to see
the man, Brazos heard him suddenly pitch and thresh, and
Trakken flopped back almost upon him.

"Two rattlers just behind me!" Trakken pawed at Brazos'
feet like a drowning man.

"Well, their big cousin is right in front of me!" Brazos
kicked off Trakken's frenzied pawing with impatient anger.
"Damn it, get off me till I use this Colt."

The slug bounced the coiled gray mass off the ground.
The rattler slithered, thrashed, and disappeared bleeding into
cover. Brazos had crawled only another body length before
he heard the wild sounds behind that told him the worst had
happened. Trakken had come to his limit of sanity.

Whether it was the rattlesnakes, or the trapped and tortured sensation that finally broke Trakken's mind, he would
never know. Some of both, perhaps; plus the exhaustion
and days-old strain of the chase. Trakken screamed like a
trapped panther. Brazos twisted to look over his shoulder
and saw the gaunt man fling out his arms and flounder upright, trying to run.

"No, Trakken!"

Trakken flung his head back, snarling. His eyes had
turned crazy wild. He gave an insane squall and threw himself full against the maze of bristling yucca daggers, as if he
meant to bull his way out of them. Stunned by the horror of
what he was witnessing, Brazos watched helplessly as Trakken flung himself this way and that, beating at the spikes
with his hands, recoiling from one set of deep stabs immediately into another. Brazos saw Trakken's hands spurt red,
then his face. He became a floundering mass of stabbed red
flesh, flailing at his thousand enemies. The gaunt bleeding
body unbelievably made a short distance of horrible progress
through the spikes. Brazos saw him pitch sightless and bloody
into the final ghastly plunge upon a piercing wall of daggers.
There he slumped, impaled and twitching as his life flowed
out. Brazos buried his head, sick.

He crawled again in the tight world of pain. Dusk came
early within his twisting tunnel. He crawled in the dark

shadows, remembering Trakken and what would happen to a
man who let himself go crazy enough to start fighting it. He
crawled when the gloom deepened and crawled when all
light died out, and crawled thereafter in blackness. He bellied
through the mile-wide Valle de Cuchillos. Just a mile, but
made of inches. A night of Apache torture, the chunk of hell
that all Texas claimed no human could enter and come out
again with enough blood and sanity left to tell it. He bellied
through hell like the other scaly and crawling things under
the spines, his mind and body numb. He crossed, and came
out to the open rocks at sunup.

He walked into Torrey's two days later after following
the Concho where it cut through the Cuchillos, still alive and
sane enough to know when Willow and Risa set in to doctoring him in the shack.

"Any word yet, from Seale?" he kept asking. Whatever the
answer was, he always passed out before he could understand it.

XIV

Bartolo furnished mustangs, rifles, ammunition, and rations
for their journey to the crucial rendezvous in the cliffs at
the head of the Valle de Cuchillos. He shrugged off their
thanks. "Man's life hanging on this."

Moss said, "You're not saying much about Captain Spide.
Heard anything of their bunch? You know damn certain we
stand to meet trouble every foot through the badlands.
They jumped Teche and me before we knew it—that's the
kind of country it is up there. Would have murdered us on
the spot if it hadn't been for Brazos."

Bartolo looked unblinkingly into distance. "There's an old
holeup camp used by Mexican army scouts, about where
you've been told to go. If some chief that stands in with the
Spider and Mexicans has got your man, and wants the gold
bad enough to sell him back to you, I would guess they'll
bring him to that place. Somewhere about there, I'd expect
Captain Spide to head you off. He would know that if
Seale McCloud goes free his own days are ended in Texas."

They waited, but Bartolo seemed finished. No, he was
working something else over in his mind. Finally he muttered, "Hear there's a Ranger patrol headed this way. Maybe
you can get some help."

Brazos said dryly, "Happens the Rangers and I aren't on speaking terms."

Bartolo nodded as if this was no news to him. "Republic of Texas not on speaking terms with your pa, either, is it? The politicians will look like fools down at Austin if it turns out he's a trade prisoner. Instead of taking life easy in Mexico City like some claim he's done by turning traitor."

"Any idea who started putting out that talk?" Brazos prompted.

Bartolo cocked a shaggy brow. "Can't you guess?"

"The Spider?"

Bartolo made a grimace that they took for an affirmative. The old man eyed Brazos. "You're going?"

"Why not?"

"Looks like you've been put through a meat grinder."

"Aw, he's all scabbed up nice," Moss put in. "Those two women doctored him good. That part-Indian one that Wid's took a shine to, and Risa Driscoll. Red here's fit again, too. Only one not able to travel is Wid."

"And it's killing him," Red added. Red was as keyed up as any of the others, as time came to head north. He had been sorely disappointed when Bartolo had told him there was no rumor of a prisoner by the name of Ben Myrick, Red's brother. But Red clung to a crazy hope that if they found Seale, they might find others, too.

Brazos had a final moment with Risa before they left the settlement. The failure of getting the Union documents to the Texas government had been bad news to him and his brothers. All of them felt plagued by their sense of obligation to the Republic. Risa had sadly related the story, revealing her own miserable feeling of guilt in her father's failure.

"I want to make it clear," Brazos told her now, "that I don't hold anything against you for what happened." Seeing the anguish in her made him add, "Or against Dr. Driscoll, either. I hope the militia didn't keep him prisoner. You've had trouble enough."

She asked in a burst of hope, "Is it too late? When we get back, could the information still be told to President Houston?"

"That's the first thing we'll do, of course. Wid and Teche and I have already agreed on that. Sam Houston will be knowing what the documents contained as soon as we can get there. Risa—thanks for the way you've taken care of me these past days. I was a right bloody mess when I stumbled in—"

"You should thank Willow. A wonderful doctor—"

"Wid thinks so. Man has a way of falling for a pretty nurse when he's sick. Did I mention your name when I was out of my head?"

"No, Brazos—"

"Well, I was thinking—"

"All you ever mumbled about was Trakken and snakes—"

"Enough to crazy a man, for a while. But I always came back to thinking of you, knowing it was you looking after me."

She murmured, "It was you I fastened my mind to, all those long terrible hours in the Spider's wagon—"

"They're waiting for me."

"Brazos—"

In her anxiety, she grasped his arm, raising her glance fearfully to search his face, until he felt hot under the distant watching of the others, and pulled himself free. There seemed nothing else for either to say. She knew his suspense was a great weight on this fateful day, that both of them, and everyone, were on edge with the showdown so near. Moss, Teche, and Red had swung into their saddles. Moss called to him to come on. He gave Risa a last look meaning reassurance, not quite sure what he did mean, or feel. He tightened the strappings of the leather band that held the gold and adjusted his rifle boot and other saddle gear, before raising his foot to the stirrup.

"You and Willow take care of Wid," he said. She stood aside. The breeze rippled her loosely hanging dress, borrowed from Willow. Her black hair was neatly combed and parted, her dark hands clasped. When he looked back from the settlement's edge she still stood there, a small waif lonely in the weeds. Willow and Wid came to the shack opening, and he knew how Wid was suffering at seeing them go without him. Brazos caught up with the others.

They rode with extreme caution over the route to the former meeting place with the first messengers. The route angled north from there to the head of the Cuchillos for the next rendezvous. Moss led the extra horse, saddled for the man they hoped would be riding it on their return.

Now they broke up into single scouting parties with rifles in their hands, remembering how quickly the Spider's men had waylaid Moss and Teche. They rode in sweaty tension, fearful of being stalked, each scanning his part of the wild terrain for any sign of movement. If the Spider's bunch lay in waiting, there were a dozen shielded places to the mile where the ambush could break. The place of the twin red-sand spires came into view just before sundown. There had been no sight of any moving life except the snakes, jack rabbits, and coyotes. Yet Brazos had known the feel of unseen eyes for the past hour. They dismounted in a mesquite-clogged ravine at the foot of the two giant rock needles.

Not one of them knew what to expect at this point, and each tried to conceal his high-honed edge with extreme effort. The strain, though, showed through pretense. Teche tried hardest to disguise his tension.

"Lovely place for a picnic," he said with forced lightness. "We must bring the girls here for an outing."

A horse snorted. The men jumped, whipping their rifles toward the ponies. Red grunted, "Just a jack rabbit."

They explored and located every boulder, cactus clump, and cut within range, every possible point for an ambush. Trouble would start after sundown. Anybody murder-bent could crawl up mighty close, the way the brush and rocks made confused shadows. While Brazos waited unmoving in his cedar clump, the sun settled out of sight. A purple cover softened the ugly land into false velvet. Their hiding places dimmed out of sight from one another. He felt completely alone. His blood pumped wildly. Somewhere in the covering dusk out there his father might also be waiting. If he was, what a fateful waiting that would be for him! Two years of brutal captivity funneled into this lonesome hour of hope, of not knowing. Seale would be wondering as Brazos wondered, if *they* were out there in the night. If his boys were waiting beyond the next ravine or thorny knoll. Brazos felt his throat dry up. His chest ached against the surge of blood under his ribs.

A horse fought its stake rope. Brazos clasped his rifle stock hard. Then, one of the others—Moss, he thought, who was in the boulders off to the southwest—gave the low soft whistle on his knuckles, thrice repeated. The innocent call of a dove.

Brazos, Teche, and Red started cautiously moving from their scattered hiding places to Moss's position.

Moss spoke against Brazos' ear and Brazos relayed it to the others. "Down the ravine. Somebody's down there. Can't see him now. Keep quiet and wait."

After what seemed an age of straining against the darkness and silence, a voice sounded and the words came in careful exploration from the distant shadows. "I come in peace, *amigos*. Are you here with gold to pay for a white man?"

Moss called, "We are."

"Walk this way, *amigos*. Leave your rifles, come to where I am."

Teche was viciously opposed to leaving their rifles. "Could be a trap."

"Damn it, we have to do it *their* way!" Moss growled. "Hold your hand guns down by your legs so they won't show."

Brazos had already started, ignoring Teche's protest. This moment was what they had been working toward for a full year. He throbbed with hope and the compulsion to move.

The man in the darkness stood apart from the cedars. His words were those of an English-speaking Cherokee. Two other shadowy figures were visible at some distance behind this one. The spokesman called that they were near enough, to listen carefully. They were to continue down the ravine in which they now stood, one hour from now. Afoot. They were to come without arms of any kind, bringing the gold. At the appointed place, they would be met by a Comanche and a Mexican. There, the transaction would be completed.

The trio faded back into the night with only a rustle of departing sound.

"It's coming off!" Brazos gritted. "We're going to get him, Teche!"

"We've still got the Spider to contend with, even if this pans out."

Moss, the old campaigner, tried to be matter-of-fact. "Now let's don't nobody start countin' chickens. This is tricky and we don't know what we're buttin' into exactly. We're pretty close to something, though. I hope it's what we came after. Just so there's not a last-minute bobble of this thing." His strain for matter-of-factness didn't quite hold. His voice broke a little on the husky emotion of his tension. Brazos hardly dared to trust his own tongue. He listened to Teche who spoke in nervous harshness.

"I don't hold for going down there without guns. That's too much like suicide and I'm against it—"

Red cut in with his own worry. "I been in the wilds a lot of my life and when I *feel* spied on, usually turns out redskins or Mexicans on my tail. Anybody but me feel that way now?"

Moss agreed. "I got the feel that somebody's stalking us from the ridge up there."

Brazos seethed with the compulsion to proceed, to disregard all things except the big one. He hugged his bag of stolen gold, and his rifle, chaffing against the talk. He stared into the night where the messengers had vanished as if to search out the answer by sheer strength of will. His own burning intent welled up in words. "The Spider was the man who traded the prisoners. If he's stalking us now, it only saves what I aim to do later—find him. The Spider represents the whole Mexican government of barbarians, far as I'm concerned. I started up here to find one man. Now it's two. I hope it's Pa first, and Captain Spide soon after. Whichever comes first, though, is the way it will be. Now I'm going up yonder with the gold and find out what we waded through hell to get to. Don't pussyfoot and don't try—"

"For God's sake, boy, nobody's pussyfootin'!" Moss tried to calm him. "We're all of the same mind. That right, Teche? Red?"

"For Spide, yes!" Teche snapped. "If not with a bullet, then a blade to his guts, and if we've got no knife, then our hands will do. Whichever of us can get to him first—"

"Seems like you're off the scent," Red objected. "The prisoners—"

"Goddam this palaver!" Brazos snarled. "We—"

"Hold it now, boy—"

But the caucus was turning into a low-pitched nervous babble by now, and it was a no-good thing. Brazos turned away in disgust for the harangue and the delay, and started a stalk into the jaws of the brushy ravine. Only showed how keyed up they were, his storming mind tried to say. Emotions and the tensions of the hour were getting the best of reason. God only knew what they were walking into, and here they were heading to the final crucial minute all crossways, confused and jittery as a flock of quail.

He slowed his steps. Sounds of the plodding progress of the others came on. Once more they walked in close file in the narrow cut.

Moss growled to him. "Hold a minute. Pretty near there, I'd guess. We better decide about what we're going to do. Keep our guns or leave them. I still think there's somebody moving with us up there on the rim."

Brazos stopped. "I say we each hide our hand guns on us. Leave our rifles."

That is how they finally proceeded over the last dark stretch of stony creek bottom beneath the starlit, rocky spires: revolvers within their shirts, rifles hidden back in the bushes.

They slowed and spread out when sound came from the shadows ahead. The weak light showed where the ravine flattened into a loose stand of mesquite saplings. Shadows moved there. Two figures detached themselves from the tree forms and approached.

The formalities were brief, and over more quickly than any had anticipated. A voice asked in Spanish if they had come to trade gold for a prisoner. Brazos showed the bag and rattled the gold. There was a snatch of low discourse between the two shadows in mixed Mexican and Indian phrases. The Spanish-speaking man called, "One advance now. With the gold."

Brazos stepped forward. His hand clutched the moneybag in a sweaty grip. He felt the weight of the Colt bulging his shirt. The night rang in his ears with the shrilling knowledge of the delicate fact at last in process of accomplishment. The figure in the dark edged out to meet him. Brazos stopped.

He tried to keep his brain clear in spite of the way blood hammered it. Moss, Teche, and Red waited close behind him in their own sweaty suspense. He found a will beyond his emotions to make his voice hold steady.

"I will place the gold on the ground between us. You will bring up the prisoner. As he walks forward from you, you will advance and pick up the money. You wish to count it first? It is near one thousand dollars."

The other hesitated, then said, "Very well, *señor.*" He spoke next in the Comanche tongue. The Indian drifted back out of vision. Brazos advanced half the distance to the lone man and placed the gold in a star-flecked spot of light. He withdrew, moving backward. The wait then, only minutes, seemed the longest of all. Something tore at his mind. Suppose his father could *not* walk forward?

Someone moved close behind him, breathing hard, and he knew it was Teche. He wondered if Teche was praying, as he was, in sudden tormenting fear, that Seale had not been mutilated or physically broken by captivity.

Shadows moved again but the silence was unbroken. Brazos and the others tried to stare the darkness apart for their first straining look at what was coming. The Comanche glided on, guiding the other shadow beside him. Then the Comanche slowed and the other figure slowly came on. The waiting Mexican fell in beside him. Still the dim light was too meager to show more than the darker blobs of their bodies.

Brazos saw the rest in the snail-slow motion of an interminable dream. The Mexican stopped, reached down for the bag of gold. The other figure stumbled on, slowly, as a man seeking his way in a strange dark room. Now the first foggy outline of him began to form for Brazos. He made out the bent, wasted figure, the long-haired head twisted sidewise for peering hard at the night. Brazos saw that, and the ragged clothes, the deep sunken eyes. He heard the man's labored breathing that turned into a mumbling low wail, incoherent in an outburst of crazed gladness.

Brazos felt his legs propel him forward, wooden from the emotions that drained him of strength. As he moved to greet his father, almost afraid to see what time had done to him, he tried to say something, meaning to call "Seale! Seale!" but the words choked him. Mist shrouded his eyesight.

The prisoner, though, did not falter in the final few steps. He burst into a gibberish of thanks and overflowing jubilation, and began falling upon all of them, Brazos, then the others, with a flood of wild mumbling thanks for his deliverance.

By the time Teche, then Moss, had pushed him off with low oaths, Brazos was seized with a sickness that made the night and the shadows dip and swim about him. Two things he had seen, the old fire scars on the stranger's face, and the pitiful joy spilling from shrunken eyes that were not Seale McCloud's.

This broken human wreckage of Mexican and Comanche brutalities, whoever it once had been, had never been their father.

Brazos called hoarsely. "You have brought the wrong man. This one we have never seen before. We have come for Seale McCloud."

The consternation was audible from the Mexican and Comanche, who went into low talk. This came to an end when the Mexican called there was a mixup, that the right man soon would be brought up. They would return the one mistakenly delivered.

"Do you mean that you have Seale McCloud nearby?"

"That one, *si*. And others. The Indians were not sure of names nor how many were to be ransomed. You have no gold for this one?"

"Only for Seale McCloud," Brazos replied. "But this is an old man, with not long to live. If there is none who will buy him, I ask that you let him stay free. You have nothing to gain by returning him to captivity."

"That we cannot do." The Mexican had maintained a surprisingly respectful tone throughout. He said, "I will oblige you to walk him back here to me."

The prisoner, who had hunkered beside Brazos, turning his long-haired head first one way and another, began to realize that his liberation had been short-lived. As Brazos reached for his arm, fighting his own repulsion for what had to be done, the old man broke into the hysterics of pleading. This sent Moss and Teche into a concerted, angry appeal again to the Mexican. But the captors appeared unmoved.

Brazos muttered, "I'm sorry. We cannot do anything for you."

He led the struggling, weakened old frame forward and the Mexican reached for him, roughly pressing him on to the Comanche as if relaying a sack of bones. The old one faded into the night, still struggling, still calling back his entreaties.

The scene was enough to unnerve them all. Brazos kept hearing Teche's low curses and Moss's throaty rumble. Red Myrick had stayed strangely silent. Something in his manner caused Brazos to turn and peer sharply at him.

"Something the matter, Red?"

Myrick was shaking. They had to strain to catch his words. "That was my brother. Maybe he recognized me, maybe not. But I know it was him. What's left of him."

Moss muttered in pain. "Sorry, Red."

Brazos grasped Red's arm. "We'll get him. We'll manage it somehow." Damn it, there was only so much gold. Red had come empty-handed, taking his chances. Still, it was a sickening thing to do, sending the old one back. But Red was not finished yet. He appeared to be thinking hard.

"He said something," Red muttered. "When he fell on my neck. All that gibberish—but these words he whispered dif-

ferent. I'm trying to remember just how they sounded. It
was like he was trying to tell me something—"

"For God's sake, *what?*" Teche demanded.

"Near as I heard 'em," Red muttered solemnly, "he said
something in my ear like 'spiders all over the ridge.' I
damn sure heard the 'spiders' part, I can swear to that and
something else. Damned if he didn't lift my knife off me!"

Each of them turned to search into the high black void
of the ravine ridge. Only the silhouetted crags showed in the
night sky. Moss said, "He was smarter than we took him for.
That was a warning. The prisoners back yonder know
there's an ambush set for us."

Brazos had his Colt out of his shirt. "In that case, we're
standing in the dead middle of the trap we've been expecting."

"Push on down the ravine," Moss ordered. "Let's don't
stay in one place making sittin' corpses. We're going to get
Seale and then get set for the Spider."

XV

Now it was too late to go back for the rifles.

Anyhow, to show arms would violate the conditions set
by the Mexican negotiator and each knew with bleak certainty that the ransom act, at best, was in ticklish balance.
Whole thing, thought Brazos, was like walking a tightrope
across a gorge and not knowing what moment a nervous hand
might slash the knot. Dealing with a mixed set of Mexican
and Comanche representatives was juggling dynamite, any
way they went at it. So they had to reason that any bobble at
this stage would jeopardize Seale. And themselves.

But as Moss had said, they were sittin' corpses, bunched
there with only hand guns, in case Spide's outlaws jumped
them, either before or after Seale was delivered. In that momentary lapse, with their attention shifting between the far
end of the ravine and the brush rim above, Red Myrick
muttered, "Prisoners must have got wind of the Spider. My
brother was tryin' to warn us. Even if we get Seale now, we
still got hell to wade."

Then he said something else. "Reckon I'll not be retreatin'
with you. Not with Ben down yonder and a chance atall at
gettin' him. You-all go on when Seale shows. I'll have my
try."

They could understand Red's feeling. Brazos stared at the dark tangle ahead. "Maybe your brother's got a scheme of his own, Red. That knife—must have been some reason he slipped it."

Moss again spoke a hoarse order to move on. They spread and advanced down the inky cut. Figures showed again in the growth ahead.

The Spanish-speaking one called, "We have the right man, now. You will come forward with the gold, as before."

Moss prompted, "Do it easy, Brazos. They'll be skittish. Red, you and me don't look at nothing but the rim up there."

Brazos gritted, "For God's sake don't move a finger till we've got Seale."

He walked slowly into a small opening and placed the bag in a rocky spot where a weak patch of sky silver came through. Two shadows floated in like drifting cedars. He heard his own hard breathing, and that of Teche who had pushed close behind him. The shadows moved infernally slow and his eyeballs hurt, so hard did he strain to see. His heart hammered crazily. He thought, *the goddam Mexican, he would make it slow and painful.*

Suddenly, almost in his ear, Teche called out harshly, unable to control his tension: "Tell us now—is it you, Pa?"

The two shadows came on a few steps over the rocks and bottom growth. Now Brazos could see them in better outline. The taller of the two slowed and lifted his head. His shoulders squared broad to the night. The words that came back answering Teche made Brazos' heart plunge as though it was knocking his ribs loose. It was his memory, rather than the dreamlike present, hearing that voice, the old tone booming deep and powerful in its old reassurance.

"It sure is, boys! Seale McCloud here, and right proud to see you."

Brazos said chokingly, "Keep coming, Pa," and Teche, "This way, Pa."

The Spaniard stopped when he reached the bag. Seale Mc-Cloud came on in short strides, head held high as he peered against the curtain of night. Now he was half a dozen steps past the Spaniard.

In a nightmarish staring at the slow action unfolding now, Brazos saw other movements of men in the distant edge of darkness from whence Seale had come. The main body of the captors and the other prisoners, he thought. His mind kept pleading, *God, don't let 'em try to pull a trick at this stage!*

Seale was now alone, walking ahead, only a few steps away. As if information had to be passed quickly in that crucial second, Seale said low and tightly: "Listen, now. About a dozen of 'em back of me, and four tied-up prisoners. The captives are going to make a break. Help 'em if you can. Don't shoot them by mistake—"

So Seale McCloud came out of captivity. Erect, unafraid, already dominating the night with just the force of his bodily presence. And with a scheme on him for striking back at his captors in the moment of his own liberation. He came abreast of Brazos. He paused and stared hard. Brazos felt his arm gripped with trembling fingers. Seale muttered feelingly, *"Boy!"* and moved on, to Teche, with the same touch, the same one low-whispered word that conveyed everything to his sons.

Teche mumbled, "Hello, Pa, are you all right?"

"All right, son."

Brazos said urgently, "We think we're ambushed somewhere above, Pa."

"You are," Seale said softly. "Captain Spide's bunch is known to be around. Watch it, now. Do what you can for my friends back there when they break loose." Seale moved on a few steps. "That Wid over there?"

"No, sir, I'm Red Myrick."

Then Brazos heard his father's low, "Hello, Moss." And Moss's voice crack between a laugh and a choke, "Howdy, Seale. Wid's back at Torrey's. Everything's all right, Seale."

Red Myrick said, "Somebody movin' up on the rim!"

Then for a short space of time there were no words and no movement at all, as they wondered desperately what to do next. Brazos' brain tried to tell him that here was uncertainty and that it could be fatal. Habit was strong. All of them were waiting instinctively for Seale to command. But he was in no shape to do so, Brazos realized. The responsibility was theirs, not his, to get out of the trap. His mere presence free and within their ranks had stunned them, in a way, had made them hesitant and fumbling for a moment. Because of this indecision, Brazos thought, the whole mission might be caught in disaster.

"Let's get it straight, Pa—quick! The other prisoners are going to break and run this way? You mean we should wait for that? Hadn't we better edge back up the ravine? Our rifles—"

"Old Ben Myrick's got a knife. Before he's tied up again

he aims to cut the binds of the others. They'll try to grab Indian knives or rifles, whatever they can get to, and run this way. When they get to here, the Comanches will be hot after them and I want us to make a stand together."

"We just got hand guns," explained Moss.

"Range will be close," said Seale. "Who can spare me a knife?"

Moss whispered, "All right, take cover. Red, keep watch on the rim there. Now, when the captives get to here, rest of us come out and get us a Comanche apiece."

The tumult broke in the far darkness of the ravine. A redskin yelled and a gun blast cut his yell short. They heard the crashing run of men in the brush. The far end of the arroyo boiled in movement. The first low-bobbling figure broke into their vision. He yelled, "Hold your fire up there!"

Seale called, "Come on, boys—keep running!"

The captives came on. Then a new flurry of sounds broke above the floor on the cut.

"Look up on the ledge!" Teche called. "Spider's crowd!"

The new sounds overhead mixed with the oncoming commotion of the captives' break through the cut. The ridge above jumped alive with dark forms sliding downgrade. Moss, who was nearest to the slope, fired and a form pitched to the rocky bottom.

The four prisoners floundered nearer in the brush and Seale called out, directing them. Brazos leveled his Colt, straining to catch sight of the first pursuers as the four bunched captives labored past his hiding place. He saw the oncoming outline of a feather-crested head and the long lance poised for the throw. He fired point-blank into the coppery chest. This one fell headlong, upsetting the next hard behind him. Brazos saw Teche whip his knife high then plunge it down. He wheeled back, firing at the third pursuer. Teche crouched beside him and his gun blasted in Brazos' ear.

The arroyo churned in confusion. Brazos thought he saw Indians in combat with men who were none of his party. Startled, and elated, he saw that the Spider's force—now in the ravine—was being attacked by the confused Comanches and Mexicans. Both sets of them had been tricked by the melee in the darkness. Teche breathed, "They don't know who's who in this mess!"

Knives, tomahawks, and clubbed rifles thudded. Men went down. Brazos and Teche held their fire, for the offspring

conflict was taking care of itself. Sounds of the bloody struggle and then of flight, faded northward down the dry creek.
The arroyo became silent as abruptly as it had erupted in
mixed-up battle. The bodies of the dead sprawled darkly in
the rocks and upon the thick thorn brush. Brazos and Teche
stood. Moss and Red made their way across.

Seale called from nearby, "Prisoners all accounted for
over here. Rest of you all right?"

Brazos and Teche were unscathed. Moss said he had a
knife cut, not bad, and Red Myrick admitted to a bullet sting
in his leg.

Peering as he went, Brazos moved among the dwarf cedars
and greasewood clumps, wondering if the Spider's body
might be among those visible. With his Colt ready, his
course took him a short distance away from the others, but
he found no sign of Captain Spide, and none of the Mexican
who had taken the gold. He was about to turn back when a
movement bent the catclaw maze dead ahead. He advanced
slowly, expecting to find a wounded man. The brush parted.
A shaggy form bounded up with a rifle spitting flame and the
bullet plucked at Brazos' hatbrim.

He would have known the thick-bodied figure and hair-
covered face in even less light. He smashed two quick shots
at the Spider, but his target vanished down into the brush.
Plunging toward that spot, watching for Spide to move again,
Brazos yelled over his shoulder, "The Spider—this way!"

He stalked the faint movement of something winding unseen through the tangle. He fired at the next bend of the
branches, a wild shot into a dark void, and kept beating
through the thorny growth. The Spider fired from out of
sight and the bullet fanned hot past Brazos' head.

Now the stalking went on by sound. The arroyo was grave-
yard still. The Spider had stopped. Both waited.

At a slight sound behind him, Brazos jerked. He cursed
the darkness. Maybe all the survivors of the Spider's force
and the Indian delegation had not retreated. Just one of 'em,
alive in hiding here, would be one too many. Brazos called
urgently toward the sound at his back: "Teche? Moss?"

A voice came calmly, "Seale, here. Keep him covered, son."

"You armed, Pa?"

"Well enough. A knife."

He had to watch ahead. Movement angled off in the brush.
Brazos pushed toward it through waist-high thorn bushes.

Captain Spide bounded up like a burly ape from the tangle. Thin light from an open sky patch gave a ghostly sheen to his bewhiskered ugliness, to his raised rifle. A trapped animal snarl started from the whiskery nest of his mouth. Brazos triggered, and sickened when the Colt hammer clicked on emptiness.

Something whispered past his ear like a wing flutter. The Spider's rifle streaked blue fire skyward toward the mesquite tops, and then the rifle itself flew upward as if the whiskered one had crazily thrown it at the clouds. Pale light had struck silvery upon the whirling blade that flashed from behind Brazos and stayed now to its hilt in the Spider's throat.

The man's heavy weight sank into the thorns to the bubbling of gargled blood. The thorns he would never feel. Brazos began reloading the Colt with numb fingers. He heard Seale at his back.

"A good throw you made, Pa."

Seale touched his shoulder. "Let's go home, son."

XVI

Three days later they came in sight of Torrey's Post. Travel had been painful and slow. The liberated captives, in various stages of crippledness and sickness, rode the mounts and the McClouds walked. By now, Seale, Ben Myrick, and the others had filled in their liberators with an account of their long captivity, from Perote Prison near Mexico City to the camps of the Comanches above the Caprock. All the dealings had been handled by Captain Spide, who, they said, was Santa Anna's chief spy in Texas. Seale, in turn, had listened avidly to news of his family, the state of things at home and over Texas. They had told him of the stolen documents, the whole story. At one point, Seale had said triumphantly: "That's nearly the best news of all, next to knowing you and the girls are all right. Means the Republic's going to be able to hold out—we'll never have to submit to annexation. Brazos, get the facts to Sam Houston just as soon as you can take out of here!"

So Seale had not changed, they saw. He was a free man again, the man whose obsession was that Texas, too, would forever be free.

The tattered, weary foot contingent and the long-starved

captives perked up with new life when finally they saw the bleak outlines of the Torrey shacks on the flat above the Concho.

"Welcome party's coming." Moss pointed.

Brazos and the others watched the approaching dust of riders. He found himself hoping that Risa Driscoll—and, as a sheepish second thought, Wid, too—might be with the party. The dust materialized into a strung-out formation of six men. Moss squinted. "Looks like the Rangers. That's Jack Hays."

The Ranger commander dismounted. He walked about, taking in the state of the liberated captives, shook hands with Seale and Ben Myrick, and then squatted to his heels to have a smoke.

"Glad to see you all look at least half-way healthy. Tell me about it."

When the Rangers had heard the story of their fight and escape from the rendezvous, he studied his smoke and said, "Sorry we were a little late. Meant to help you, if we got here in time."

Seale said, half-humorously, "The government would help *me,* Jack?"

The young captain grinned wryly. "Not the gov'ment, Mr. McCloud. Just me. Jack Hays, and my men."

"Thought I was playing it loose with the Mexico bigwigs, down at the City. Spilling secrets all over the place, being the sold-out traitor."

"That's Austin says that," Hays corrected. "Mainly those you opposed so damned stubborn on annexation. No, I guess you wasn't living very high with the Mex, if you was up the Caprock in a Comanche camp."

He turned to look at Brazos. "How's the stolen government document business these days?"

"Everything's damned good!" Brazos grinned. "Your job's secure, too, Jack. There's not going to be any annexation!"

"You still going to see the gov'ment down at Austin?"

"Soon as I can get there."

Hays stood. "Our supply wagon's at the post. We're going to take you folks back home. Wagon for the two women and Wid and such of these captives that ain't up to the ride. Escort for all of you. Guess that's the least we can do, since we got here tardy for the fireworks."

Teche repeated, "Two women, you say? Who beside Miss Driscoll?"

"Been talking to Wid, so I guess I got news you don't know. The widow that's been taking care of him—name of Willow. Seems that Wid is taking her back south with him."

Seale swung his head in question. Teche murmured, "Why that damned old Wid! Fell for a woman!"

The Rangers furnished lead mounts and the party rode into Torrey's Post at sundown. Brazos saw the gesture of greeting from Bartolo, his granite cracked by a smile; saw in a moment Wid coming at a hobbling run, and how Seale swung off his horse to embrace his eldest; and then he saw nothing but Risa Driscoll waiting shyly in the background and being ogled by all the Rangers. Through the tumult of the dismounting and talk and dusty commotion he edged his way and stood before her. He reached his hands and she took them, and he meant to say something. Whatever it was got no farther than his throat. Risa buried her dark head into his chest and the small form of her shook with a sob of gladness.

After a time, Brazos, still holding her, looked down and said, "Come over here. I want you to meet Seale."

Risa whispered, "It will be the proudest moment of my life."

Two weeks later, Brazos sat across from a gray-haired, thoughtful man in an office in the Secretary of State's department in Austin. He was dressed in town clothes, with all the signs of the hard trail nearly faded off him, and he was bent on discharging a delayed duty. The doctor who had been expected to deliver the information had been detained by the militia, he explained, though he was now back at the McCloud ranch and trying to make up for his failure by full-time doctoring of Seale and Wid McCloud.

"What I have to report came in some Union documents I had occasion to read," Brazos went on. The gray-eyed assistant secretary leaned back, touched his fingers together and nodded thoughtfully for Brazos to proceed. "We've got more backing to stay out of annexation than anybody around here supposes," said Brazos, plunging to it. "The Union is in a muddle over this in more ways than one. Here's how it is, and I wanted the Secretary and President Houston to know this, as soon as possible—"

The man nodded shortly. "The Secretary has instructed me to hear your report. You can be sure he and the President will know immediately."

So Brazos related the information from the documents in great detail, and his words huskied a little as he got to the key points that indicated England would do everything to back Texas as an independent republic.

"So we have only to hold on a little longer," he concluded. "We've got the Union and Mexico both on the run. We can come out being even a bigger nation than the Union—plenty of support from England—our western boundary running clear to the Pacific—"

The thoughtful eyes behind the desk lowered themselves. For a time there was no comment. Then the assistant spoke slowly, looking not at Brazos but out at the city through the window.

"I appreciate your trouble in bringing this information," he said soberly. "But I am afraid I have bad news for you— bad, that is, if that's the way you wish to see it. And from what I've heard of the McClouds, you will see it as bad." He cleared his throat. "The Secretary had assumed that what you wanted to report would be about what you've told me. He and the President have decided that I am to be honest with you, and request your confidence. McCloud—" The gray eyes twinkled a little but the mouth stayed grim. "Most of the information you—er—happened upon, was information planted by our own Secretary and President. Mr. Houston, in fact, has authored much of it. And has been doing so for months. Politics and diplomacy are strange animals, young man. They would be specially strange to you. But there is much at stake. It is enough that I tell you that we are jockeying for the best terms possible from the Union, when annexation time comes, as it inevitably must. President Houston, in all frankness, engineered most of the rumors you referred to, and our envoys in Washington managed to let Union agents 'steal' the correspondence. Do you follow me?" He leaned forward and said with tightening fists: "We've had one turndown from the U.S. Senate, you know. Now, the Union is a lot more eager for annexation than before—and President Houston is shrewdly pulling strings and playing coy, to get the best conditions possible when the treaty stage is reached. So, I am sorry you have been to so much trouble—that this has weighed so heavily upon you. But now you know that most of what you have 'discovered' in the Union papers was manufactured right here in this department."

Brazos felt sweaty in every thread of his dress-up clothes.

He worked his hatbrim with dead fingers. "Then it's—it was all a hoax?"

"You might call it that."

The assistant saw him to the door and dropped a kindly hand on his shoulder. "Don't let your family take it too hard, McCloud. It's all going to work out for the best for Texas." Brazos nodded bleakly. The man added, "And the Secretary and President Houston both ask that you deliver their felicitations to your father. They regret certain—er, that some misunderstandings have occurred in the past. It may be we have made a mistake in regard to certain of the Woll prisoners and some from the Santa Fe expedition. Ah, we live in much confusion these days."

"I'll tell Pa."

All he could think, as he walked blindly through the heavy wagon and buggy traffic of the town, toward the livery barn: *The bastards! The dirty, cowardly bastards!* This news would just about kill Seale. He turned and looked back toward the capitol building and the Lone Star flag rippling on the staff above it.

In December, the U.S. Senate approved annexation of Texas and the people of the battered republic were given the year of 1845 in which to make their decision and vote their verdict. Houston had drawn amazingly favorable terms, in big concessions and big cash, most men agreed. The Mc-Clouds said there was nothing good about any of it. Seale left to electioneer with the antiannexation forces. But annexation fever went up as the Texas treasury went down, and Mexico's war threats and England's confusion did little to improve the chances of maintaining independence. The people recorded their decision to accept the Union treaty in October of that year. News of the election result came to the McCloud place a few days later and when the rider departed, the adobe was left filled with mute and disappointed people. Seale stepped to the porch and looked off across the valley's hazy distance. Risa touched the arm of Brazos, her new husband. Wid and Willow stood in the doorway, watching Seale. Teche and Ann forced tight smiles. Sabine and Neches wept. Dr. Driscoll coughed and eyed the corner cupboard where the whisky was kept.

After a little while, Seale observed their various states of sadness and tried to set them an example for taking bad news in stride. "All right," he said roughly. "We've still got a

ranch to run and cattle to work. We've survived every other
adversity the devil could throw at this outfit—I reckon we
can weather one more, even if it's being took in by a stronger tribe."

On an early February day in 1846, a messenger came
again to the McCloud homestead, this time with an official-
looking letter addressed to Seale. President Anson Jones had
succeeded Sam Houston, and the envelope had his name
scrawled across the Republic seal in black ink.

"They want us to come to the annexation ceremony in Austin, on the nineteenth," he said after reading it.

"Something I want to stay as far away from as possible,"
growled Wid.

"It's a little more than that," Seale said slowly. "They want
the whole family in a body. You boys and your wives. All of
us. Along with some others who were prisoners of the Mexicans and the Indian tribes. Something about honors and
recognition—"

They entered the crowded meeting place in Austin that
day, February 19, 1846, the whole strung-out McCloud
troupe, muscles sore from the long ride by wagon and horse-
back, the women stiff in their best calico and corsets, the
men rigidly erect and ill at ease before so many eyes and in
their tight homespun coats. They followed Seale as an official herded them through the crowd, down the aisle and to
a row of reserved benches. Seale went in first, and they filled
up the entire row, from Seale at one end to Dr. Driscoll at
the other and all the clan in between. A few nearby heads
turned and sober greetings went back and forth. "Hullo,
Seale." "Remember me at Perote, Seale?" "Hi, Wid—remember Salado Creek?" And then a speaker was trying to
quiet the buzz and after him a frock-coated gentleman arose
and the crowd stood and President Anson Jones prepared to
say the farewell words that would bring down the Texas
flag and run up the Stars and Stripes. First, though, the
President said, he wanted to recognize a special contingent
present on the occasion. Then he proceeded to pay his respects and the Republic's homage to all Texas men who had
been subjected in various circumstances to captivity at the
hands of their Mexican enemies or of the Indian tribes. He
referred to the Woll raid, the Mier raid survivors, the Santa
Fe expedition and some of the Indian raids, and called various prominent names. Toward the end, he said: "And I wish
to publicly pay my respects, on this occasion, to a good Texas

citizen, Seale McCloud, of San Antonio. We rejoice that he has been returned to his family from captivity. We are grieved if thoughtless ones in the past have erroneously and misinformedly attached a blame to that proud name, which blame, we today know ashamedly, was undeserved and unjust. He fought with valor at San Jacinto as did one of his sons at Salado. Seale McCloud, one of the last acts of the Republic of Texas is this humble gesture for making amends —to extend to you and your family our greetings, our respects, our admiration. I can only say that this was just one of several wrongs our nation has done to various individuals, in times of great stress, uncertainties, and confusion. God be with you, now, and forgive us our shortcomings. And now, my fellow-Texans—for the business at hand." The crowd went hushed. A lump seemed to come into the President's throat. His hand shook a little as it clutched a sheaf of papers.

Brazos stole a glance past Risa's set lips, saw Seale at the end of the row beyond Wid and Willow, his eagle-alert head erect, mouth tautly set beneath a line of gray clippped mustache, eyes hard on the speaker. President Anson Jones addressed the assembled Senate and House of Representatives and began to read his last address as president of a republic that was to be no more:

"The great measure of annexation, so earnestly desired by the people of Texas, is happily consummated. The present occasion so full of interest to us, and to all the people of this country, is an earnest evidence of that consummation; and I am happy to greet you as their chosen representative, and tender to you my cordial congratulations on an event the most extraordinary in the annals of the world, and one which marks a bright triumph in the history of republican institutions. A government is changed both in its officers and its organic law—not by violence and disorder, but by the deliberate and free consent of its citizens; and amid the most perfect and universal peace and tranquillity, the sovereignty of the nation is surrendered, and incorporated with that of another.

"There is no precedent for this, and henceforward 'Annexation' is a word of new import in the political vocabulary of America, to form a subject for the speculations of the Statesman and the intellectual labors of the Sage. Nations have generally extended their dominions by conquest; their march to power involving bloodshed and ruin, and their attainment of it often followed by suffering and calamity to a despairing and subjugated people. It was left for the Anglo-American inhabitants of the Western Continent to furnish a new mode of enlarging the bounds of empire, by the more natural tendency and operation of the principles of their free government. Whatever objections may have been heretofore urged to the territorial enlargement of the Union, those objections must now be regarded as overruled and as being without practical effect. Annexation is the natural consequence resulting from congenial impulses and sympathies; and the operation and influence of like sympathies and impulses are destined, as soon as can be important or necessary, to settle all conflicts in relation to the claim of the United States to any territory now in dispute on this continent.

"In accordance with the provisions of the new constitution adopted by the Convention, called by me on the fourth of July last, a State government is now perfectly and fully organized, and I, as President of the Republic, with my officers, am now present to surrender into the hands of those whom the people have chosen, the power and the authority which we have some time held. This surrender is made with the most perfect cheerfulness, and in respectful submission to the public will. For my individual part, I beg leave further to add, that the only motive which has heretofore actuated me in consenting to hold high and responsible office in this my adopted and beloved country, has been to aid, by the best exertions of such abilities as I possessed, in extricating her from her difficulties and to place her in some safe and secure condition, where she might be relieved from the long pressure of the past and repose from the toils, the sufferings, and threatened danger, which have surrounded her. I have considered annexation on favorable terms as the most secure and advantageous measure for Texas, and as affording the best prospect for the attainment of the object I had in view, and have, accordingly, in different capacities labored most assiduously to open the door in the United States to its accomplishment. In this I succeeded. I sincerely wish the terms could have been made more advantageous, more definite, and less fraught with subjects of future dispute; but as they proved entirely acceptable to a vast majority of my fellow citizens, I felt it to be my imperative duty, so soon as that fact was known, faithfully and promptly to carry into full effect the will and the wishes of the people. This I have done; and in the execution of this work, I am happy to add, I have received the cordial support and cooperation of every member of my cabinet, and of every officer of the government at home and abroad, whose services I have had occasion to employ in connection with it. Annexation has met with no impediment in Texas, nor has any been attempted by the Government; and I believe I am justified in saying that it has been accomplished in the very safest and best manner practicable, and at the very earliest possible period of time. I know of no course which could have been adopted which would have effected this object one single day earlier. In the meantime I have obtained from Mexico a formal acknowledgement of our national independence, thereby removing the principal objection to the measure on the part of the United States.

"Satisfied that the happiness and welfare of Texas are placed on a strong and secure foundation, and that she will now find many friends better qualified than myself, who will take care of her interests, the motive to which I have alluded as having actuated me in holding office, is no longer operative; and in retiring now to private life, I but indulge my individual wishes, and I lay down the honors and the cares of the Presidency with infinitely more of personal gratification than I assumed them. . . . Whatever injustice may have been done me, in moments of excitement, I indulge the belief that when correct information is disseminated in regard to my whole course, the public mind will settle down into proper conclusions, and that my fellow citizens will then judge me rightly. . . . With such a population as Texas possesses, characterized as it is with great intelligence and enterprise, and with such elements of prosperity as she now possesses, a genial climate and a fertile soil, it will be her own fault if she does not reach an importance and a social elevation not surpassed by any community on earth.

"Detailed reports from all the different Departments and Bureaus, showing the transactions of the Government since the last annual meeting of Congress are made out and will be handed to His Excellency the Governor, for transmission in due time to your honorable bodies. . . . It does not come within the province of my appropriate duty to make any suggestions or recommend any measures for your consideration. This task now belongs to another, and will, I am well satisfied, be discharged with faithfulness and ability. I may, however, express the fervent hope, which I have, that your important deliberations, commenced under such favorable auspices, may result in the promotion of the permanent welfare of the State of Texas, and that your labors may be crowned with abundant blessings.

"The Lone Star of Texas, which ten years since arose amid clouds, over fields of carnage, and obscurely shone for a while, has culminated, and, following an inscrutable destiny has passed on and become fixed forever in that glorious constellation, which all freemen and lovers of freedom in the world must reverence and adore—the American Union. Blending its rays with its sister stars, long may it continue to shine, and may a gracious Heaven smile upon this consummation of the wishes of the two Republics, now joined together in one—'May the Union be perpetual, and may it be the means of conferring benefits and blessings upon the people of all the States,' is my ardent prayer.

"The final act in this great drama is now performed: the Republic of Texas is no more."

They rode back toward San Antonio through the afternoon, up and down the still-green country, winding through the hills, and camped for the night on the Blanco River. The three wives and the younger girls and Wid and Dr. Driscoll left the wagon, the others picketed their horses, and a campfire was started.

There was not much talk. Brazos and Risa wandered off from the fire a little way, up a grassy kroll where they found Seale standing alone, his head lifted and his gaze caught by the splashy red and purple run of colors where the sun had set beyond the Llano hills.

Without turning, knowing by footstep and feel who it was behind him, Seale said as if murmuring a passing thought aloud: "Heard of a new country opening up beyond a river out west. A stream they call the Pecos. Sorta been wondering what's out there."

Brazos felt a tingling surge of interest quicken his own heartbeat, and raised his glance high to the west, too, like Seale, to see into the purpling golden distance where the sun had left its splendid trail.

Beside him, plucking at his sleeve, a brown hand insisted that he turn to look down into blue eyes, brightly shining. "A river named Pecos," murmured Risa.

He nodded, smiling in understanding. A good name, he thought, for their first son.

Will C. Brown is the pen name under which Clarence Scott Boyles, Jr., has written most of his western fiction. Born in Baird, Texas, and descended from Texas cattle-raising families on both sides, Boyle's early career was in newspaper journalism. Although he did publish a couple of Western stories in pulp magazines in the 1930s, it was first following his discharge from the U.S. Marine Corps after the Second World War that he began his writing career in earnest. Texas is the principal setting in nearly all of Boyles's Western stories, including his first novel, *The Border Jumpers* (1955), which also served as the basis for the memorable motion picture, *Man of the West* (1958) staring Gary Cooper. Dell Publishing, which reprinted this novel, selected it to receive the Dell Book Award as the best Western novel of 1955. *The Nameless Breed* (1960) won the Golden Spur Award from the Western Writers of America in the category of best Western novel and is still considered to the Will C. Brown's *magnum opus*. A trek through the mile-wide *Valle de Cuchillos*, or Valley of the Knives, is the highlight of this story, vividly and harrowingly told. In these novels, as well as in *Laredo Road* (1959), *Caprock Rebel* (1962), and *The Kelly Man* (1964), a high level of suspense is established early and maintained throughout, often by characters being pitted against adverse elements and terrain. Boyles is particularly adept at making his readers feel the heat, dust, wind, desolation, and dangers of the land in his stories. When violence does occur, it is logical and handled with restraint and brevity.